DECEPTION

Sydney Campbell

Deception

2

For all of you who came along for the ride.

Other books by Sydney Campbell:

Allie Styles Romance Series:
Temptation (Book 1)
Deception (Book 2)
Reckonings (Book 3)
Beginnings (Book 4)

Courtyard Tales of Contemporary Romance
Reawakening
Redemption
Reckless

CHAPTER ONE

It was a beautiful Sunday morning in October as I stood outside my boutique hotel in Amsterdam, contemplating the building. Boutique might have been generous – the place was incredibly narrow and had to have been tiny inside. I looked back, but my cab driver was already gone. I took a deep breath and walked through the front door.

There was no lobby, just a long desk by a narrow staircase. A sign over the desk read RECEPTION, and underneath, in smaller print, *No joints before lunch*. I rolled my eyes. Gotta love Amsterdam. I rang the bell on the desk and a short, curly-haired woman in what can only be described as a frock emerged from a door I hadn't even noticed. She looked at me and gave me a funny smile.

"Ms. Styles," she said with a thick Dutch accent.

"Yes."

I proceeded to check in, grabbed my bag, and climbed the stairs. I'd never been to Amsterdam before, but I was beginning to suspect there would be a lot of stairs involved. On the third floor, I put my key in the lock of the only door and turned the knob, but was met with resistance when I tried to push it open.

Looking in, I saw the bed blocking my way. The room was tiny. I squeezed in, dropped my bags on the one chair, and looked around. White walls, one small painting of a tree, a single bed, a chair, and a door. *Please let that lead to a bathroom.* I walked over and slid the door open. Sure enough, it was a minuscule bathroom with a sink, a toilet, a showerhead over the toilet, and a drain in the floor.

"Oh, good Lord."

I walked into the bathroom and looked in the mirror. At 31, I still looked like I was in my mid-twenties. I never knew if that was a good thing or not. Brown curly hair, a small smattering of freckles across my nose, and my too-big mouth, or at least I had always thought so. One guy had once referred to my mouth as generous. It left me with the weirdest feeling.

I washed my face quickly and changed into a fresh T-shirt and cardigan. I fixed my hair as best I could and walked out the door. I was jetlagged as hell, but if I slept then, I'd be ruined for days. Best if I stayed awake until at least dinner.

I grabbed a walking map of the city off the front desk as I headed out the door. I had no intention of doing any real sight-seeing—I was way too tired for that. But I had to walk around the city or I'd spend the entire day rehashing the morning's events.

I'd flown across the ocean to surprise Matt with a week of wild sex, only to have him surprise me by having another woman answer the door. In her underwear. He had *just* been sexting with me. The shock, combined with the jet lag, was too much and I just passed out. Right at the front door, right in front of them.

When I came to, I was on a couch, with both Matt and the leggy blond standing over me, peering anxiously into my eyes. I jumped up.

"I'm sorry," I said. "This was a mistake."

I rushed to the door where I saw my bags sitting and grabbed them. Matt raced over to me but stopped about five feet away. He looked at me, tilting his head to the side, impossible to read.

"Allie, let me explain."

"No, it's fine. There's nothing to explain. I've got to run. I, uh, have a meeting."

I stumbled trying to open the door.

"Allie! Are you okay? You just fainted. Maybe have some water…"

"I'm fine, Matt. Low blood pressure. Happens all the time. I'll get in touch, or, uh…I gotta go."

And I went. Fast. I raced down the same stairs that moments earlier had been terrifying to me. But now nothing was more terrifying than hearing Matt's explanation for whatever was going on in there.

"Allie," he called from the landing. "Just listen to me…"

I reached the street and walked as fast as I could to the corner, not stopping until I was two blocks away. Then I collapsed onto a bench and cried. What an idiot I'd been.

Coming here had been such an impulsive decision. Matt and I weren't dating. Hell, we'd only really gotten to know each other days before he left. This was a cross-Atlantic voyage based on lust. Ridiculous. Maybe I'd gotten what I deserved. He must have freaked out when I showed up on his door like that. Could I be more of a stalker?

I pulled the map out of my pocket and took a

quick look. I didn't want to study it too long. I'd traveled enough to know that tourists are taken for easy targets. And if I was honest with myself, I didn't care where I was going. I was happy just getting lost in the city. I wandered along the canals and through the side streets, and watched as four people moved a couch into a house through a third-floor window using a rope and pulley system, which I imagined was easier than trying to get it up those narrow flights of stairs.

The city was beautiful, and I loved it instantly. I was looking forward to going to the museums—especially the Rijksmuseum, the Van Gogh Museum, and Anne Frank's house. And of course, I'd check out the coffee shops, maybe wander around the red-light district... After all, I had research to do now.

I still couldn't believe it. Days before leaving on this trip, I'd submitted a piece of erotica I'd written to a new editor, and she'd hired me to produce 2000 words a week for an up-and-coming website. I was writing under a pen name, Temple Fraser, and it was the best job I'd ever had.

Writing erotica was a far cry from the restaurant reviews I'd been doing for the past five years, and I'd based my first two stories on encounters with Matt. We'd only had three. I was rapidly running out of material and had been hoping to replenish the stores this week.

I was walking down a pedestrian street, contemplating between visiting the sex shop or the waffle and crepe place when I noticed the 420 Café. Smiling to myself, I crossed the street and walked in the front door. The place was amazing, the smell of pot wafting through the air, with wood paneling, stickers adorning the walls, and low couches lining the perimeter. I picked up a menu as I took my seat, almost giddy at the possibilities.

I spent the next hour or so relaxing in the café, and then spent the next several hours people-watching along the streets of Amsterdam. I was pleasantly high and carrying a nice little stash of supplies in my purse. I figured after a good night's sleep, a combination of space cake and Van Gogh might be just what the doctor ordered to get my mind off this mess I'd gotten into.

And that's what it was. A mess. Something I'd tried so hard to avoid since breaking up with Josh, my ex. After years of "it's complicated," I just wanted something simple and reliable. Yet here I was. Why had I even come?

CHAPTER TWO

I turned the corner back onto the block my hotel was on. I figured I'd drop off my stash, shower, and find nice little tapas bar for dinner. I wasn't sure how much longer I could stay upright—exhaustion threatened to overtake me. But as I approached the hotel's entrance, my heart stopped, and I was suddenly wide awake. Matt was waiting on the front stoop.

Matt, with his dark curly hair now falling just past his ears. Clearly, he hadn't found a barbershop yet. And those sea-green eyes, looking at me as I came down the street. He stood up as I approached, and my belly did a flip at the sight of his 6'2" frame unfolding. How had he found me?

"Hey," he said.

"Hey, yourself."

"You're high. That must have been some meeting."

"There was no fucking meeting, Matt. I came here to see you. And guess what I saw?"

"You didn't see what you think you saw."

"Please."

I pushed past him and walked into the hotel lobby. He followed me in but quickly realized there was very little room. I walked straight up the stairs to my room and he followed close behind.

"How did you find me?" I asked without turning to look at him.

"There aren't too many hotels in the area. I just spent the day walking around, checking them all."

Christ, that was sweet. What was wrong with him? What was wrong with me?

"I was worried about you, Allie. And I wanted to explain."

"I told you, you don't owe me any explanations."

We had arrived at my door and I turned the key in the lock and pushed it open as far as I could.

"You're welcome to come in, but you might have to sit on the toilet."

Matt laughed and followed my lead as I squeezed through the door and crawled over the bed. He closed the door behind him. He removed my bag from the chair and sat down.

"Maja's my roommate, Allie. There's nothing going on between us."

"Roommate? You never mentioned a roommate."

"I didn't see the point. You weren't here. We're not even dating. There's nothing going on. Why bother telling you? So you'd think I was trying to make you jealous? For Christ's sake, Allie, she's gay."

That stopped me cold. It explained a lot, actually. I looked over at him, sheepishly.

"I was tired and jetlagged, and I was so excited to see you… and then she answered the door…"

He put out his hand, but let it drop on the bed without touching me. He was still uncertain, and in truth, I found it incredibly sexy. A man who understood boundaries was way hotter than any man I'd ever been with.

"I get it. I do. I'd have drawn the same conclusions. But now you know. Come home with me, Allie. Please."

I smiled.

"I'm still a little mad at you," I said.

He jumped up and grabbed my bags.

"Let's go," he said.

With that, he exited the room and practically flew down the stairs, taking them two at a time. I marveled at how quickly he'd gotten used to them. He'd only been here six weeks. True, I was jetlagged, exhausted, and high, but I got vertigo looking down.

I checked out quickly at the front desk, assuring the woman that nothing was wrong with the hotel, though maybe I should've mentioned something about the toilet/shower combo. I joined Matt in the street and together we walked slowly back to his apartment.

"She hasn't been here the whole time," Matt explained. "I'm the longest renter, but the other room in the apartment turns over every few weeks or so. Maja's from Sweden. The last guy was from Japan. It's kind of neat, actually."

"And how do you know she's gay? Did you come on to her?"

Matt laughed.

"Are you kidding? At first, I was terrified of her. Did you see her? But she and her girlfriend make it abundantly clear where their preferences lie." He paused. "You'll see."

This information didn't quite sit well with me, either.

"That's quite the setup you've got. Two women making out all the time. Must be rough."

Matt laughed again.

"I thought it would be pretty hot, too. But those two are just too much. It's nauseating."

"How long has she been here?"

Matt thought a moment before answering, rubbing his scar with his middle finger.

"Two weeks? And she leaves in a few days. How long are you here for?"

"A week."

"That's it? Well, my next roommate—Greg, I think—doesn't arrive until Thursday, so we'll have a few nights alone at least."

He smiled wickedly at me, and despite my annoyance with him, I knew I was starting to thaw. As we approached Matt's flat, however, the irritation returned. It wasn't rational, but I blamed him for my shame and humiliation that morning. And now, I had to face that Amazon woman again.

Matt opened the door and stood aside to let me in. The flat was nicely decorated in cool colours and a very minimalist design. The one exception was the sectional sofa in the living room, which was incredibly plush and comfy looking. It didn't fit the décor at all, but I'm sure every renter was happy it was there. There was one bedroom off the living room, Matt's, and then a short hallway towards the second bedroom, kitchen, and bathroom.

I barely had time to register all this before Maja jumped off the couch and raced towards us. She was dressed now, though she looked just as naked as she had that morning. She had on a pair of tight denim capris and a fitted white T-shirt. Every curve on her body showed and she knew it. With long, wavy blond hair and blue eyes, the woman exuded sex. But she also exuded something else. Warmth.

She grabbed me and folded me into her arms. Her perfume, some sort of woodsy vanilla mix, invaded my senses, temporarily stunning me into silence and she pulled away and took my face in her hands.

"Allie! I'm so sorry about earlier. Are you okay?"

I smiled shyly and stepped back, out of her reach.

"I'm fine. You're Maja, right? I'm sorry—I was just caught off guard."

Maja laughed and shook her head, her long mane of blond hair tossed about like some shampoo commercial.

"Think nothing of it. We all know it's Matt's fault, anyway."

Maja stuck out her tongue at Matt just as a petite brunette walked out of the second bedroom. She smiled at me and walked over to

Maja, snaking her arm around her waist. She fit perfectly under Maja's arm, like a little pet.

"Allie, this is Genevieve. Genevieve, Allie."

"Un plaisir," Genevieve said.

"Genevieve picked up Indian food for dinner. Why don't you two join us? I'm sure Allie is much too tired to go out to eat. It must've been a long day, what with the flight and everything."

Maja and Genevieve made their way over to the large sectional couch and started unpacking the takeout containers from the canvas bag on the coffee table.

"I'm just going to put your bags away," Matt said to me and disappeared into his room.

I wandered through the flat until I found the kitchen and searched through the cabinets and drawers, managing to find plates and cutlery. I was so tired I felt like I was on another planet. I had to focus not to stumble on my way back to the living room. Maja and Genevieve were snuggling on one side of the couch and Matt sat on the other. I placed my load down on the table and gingerly made my way around the two women to take my place in the corner seat of the couch. I was not yet ready to sit too close to Matt. As hunger and fatigue set in, the irritation returned.

Matt, sensing my mood, quickly made me a

plate and handed it over. I smiled in appreciation and dug in. Maja peppered me with questions without even waiting for answers until Genevieve gently interrupted her.

"Cherie, don't you think maybe Allie is tired? Let her just relax. We can get to know her tomorrow."

I smiled gratefully at Genevieve and resumed eating. There was an empty pit in my stomach and I couldn't possibly eat enough to fill it. Eventually I did, though, and gratefully put my plate down.

"Thank you, Genevieve. That was delicious," I said. "I picked up a little something today. Maybe I can contribute to dessert?"

I reached over for my purse and extracted my goodie bag from the 420 Café. I pulled out the space cakes and broke them into pieces on one of the empty plates. Everyone reached forward and took some. They were pretty tasty, but I knew it would be a while before they kicked in. Matt reached behind him and grabbed an ashtray off the table which contained an almost-new joint.

"Delicious, but they may take a while," Matt said, grinning. "Maybe you want to take the edge off right away?"

He lit the joint, took a few hits, and passed it to me. I took it gratefully and enjoyed a long drag. It was much better weed than we had at home, obviously. I closed my eyes and savoured the feeling of the creeping high. I opened them and turned to hand the joint to Maja, only to find her completely entwined with Genevieve, the two of them making out like a couple of teenagers.

I took another hit off the joint and kept watching. It was like they weren't even there, like I was watching a movie. The way Maja's hands held Genevieve's face while Genevieve's hands worked their way across Maja's body. They were trapped in a passionate kiss, neither of them willing to come up for air, Genevieve practically crawling into Maja's lap. I slowly licked my lips, transfixed.

Matt kicked me, hard, in the shin.

"Ouch!" I said, inadvertently.

Maja broke the kiss and looked over. I blushed as she caught me staring while simultaneously rubbing my shin. Now I was pissed at Matt all over again for embarrassing me. Fine, so maybe I had been staring. He could've been a little more subtle about informing me. But Maja didn't look upset. In fact, she looked amused.

"Are you curious?" she asked.

I blushed again, even deeper this time. Damned genes.

"I was just thinking how much easier it must be," I said.

"Not really," Maja laughed. "But it's certainly more fun."

She paused and looked at me, considering.

"Have you ever been with a woman?" she asked.

Something deep within me stirred. This evening was taking a very unexpected turn.

"No."

"Have you ever even kissed a woman?"

"No."

Maja smiled mischievously.

"Would you like to?"

With that, she untangled herself from Genevieve and got up from her seat. She walked over to where I was sitting and sat down next to me, so close our thighs were touching. My breath caught. I had no intention of making out with this woman, but the jetlag, the pot, and most of all, my still-present anger at Matt were making me think maybe a little kiss wasn't such a terrible idea.

"Maja," Matt said, finally interjecting. "Leave her alone. Like Genevieve said, she's exhausted. She's not up for your games tonight."

That was the final straw. I looked straight into Maja's eyes.

"Yes. I would."

Maja smiled, triumphant. Without giving me a moment to reconsider, she took my head in her hands and leaned towards me. She touched my lips with hers, softly, and then licked her lips before covering my mouth completely with a kiss. It was incredibly tender, and whatever fear or nervousness I might have felt vanished instantly. I melted easily into the kiss and Maja clearly took that as encouragement. She parted her lips and ran her tongue over my lower lip, waiting for an invitation. I eagerly let her in, kissing her deeply and with zero reservation.

It was so different from any kiss I'd had before. The gentleness, the *femininity*, combined with the sureness and force was incredibly erotic. Maja's mouth was no longer asking, it was taking. And I was more than willing to give. I felt her move even closer towards me, and that's when Genevieve came over and gently pulled her away.

"That's enough, ma cherie," she said.

Maja looked up at her and pouted.

"But it was just getting good," she said.

Genevieve pulled her up and away from me, shrugging her shoulders in apology. I smiled nervously, not sure how to react. I looked over at Matt, who was just sitting there staring at me, his mouth half-open. I raised an eyebrow and smirked at him before turning back to Maja.

"That was lovely, Maja. Thank you. I think I'll go to bed now."

And with that, I stood up and walked out of the living room, into Matt's bedroom, and shut the door.

CHAPTER THREE

Clever as he was, Matt didn't follow me into the bedroom. I sat down on the bed for a moment to collect myself. *That was hot.* And not at all what I had expected. I couldn't help but lament my wasted college years. I grabbed my bag, pulled out my toiletries, and put the bag away. I really didn't want to leave the bedroom to brush my teeth.

I got up and pulled a T-shirt from the pile of clean laundry stacked on Matt's dresser. The room was awfully neat. I was impressed. I peeled off my clothes, slipped on his shirt, and crawled into the bed. We'd barely said two words to each other. We were not off to a good start. But I was too tired and too stoned to do anything about it that night, so I rolled over and went to sleep.

Sometime later, I shot up out of bed and glanced at the clock. Three a.m. It would be nine p.m. at home. I'd only slept four hours, but I was wide awake, and a little disoriented. I looked around and saw Matt fast asleep next to me, on top of the covers. He looked so sweet, hair tousled and a dreamy expression on his face. He was a stomach sleeper and even though he was wearing pajamas, I could still see the outline of his muscular back through the thin cotton.

As quietly as I could, I eased myself out of bed, grabbed my toothbrush, and walked out of the room. As I passed through the living room, I spotted a half-smoked joint in the ashtray on the coffee table. That would certainly put me to sleep. I walked over to the couch and sat down, tucking my legs up under me. There was a blanket, so I wrapped it around my legs and lit the joint. I thought about what I was going to say to Matt in the morning. We had to get past this. I had to get past this. So he didn't tell me. Big deal. We had agreed to keep this casual. He had done nothing wrong.

I was almost finished the joint when I heard the soft moan come from down the hallway. I put it out and got up. It was coming from Maja's room, and her door was open. I had to pass her room to get to the bathroom, and at this point, it wasn't just about brushing my teeth—I desperately had to pee. Another moan came as I tiptoed cautiously across the hall.

"Oh, Genny..." Maja sighed.

I stood just outside the door and feeling guilty as fuck but unable to stop myself, I peered in. Both women were completely naked. Maja was lying on the bed, knees up with her legs spread. Genevieve was lying on top of her, supporting herself on her elbows as her head dipped to take Maja's nipple in her mouth.

Maja's hands were in Genevieve's hair and she was positively writhing on the bed. Genevieve rolled off her and, lying beside her, ran her hand slowly up Maja's leg.

"Genny, Genny... I want you to fuck me."

Genevieve slipped her hand between Maja's legs, rubbing her slowly with the flat of her palm. Maja's hips bucked, pressing firmly into Genevieve.

"Oh, yes..."

Suddenly, Genevieve sat up and crawled back between Maja's legs. She spread them apart slowly and then eased herself down, dipping her head as she went. Maja clutched

Genevieve's hair, moaning and squirming beneath her.

I stood there, completely mesmerized and completely turned on. I had never seen anything like this before, and even though I knew it was wrong to keep watching, I couldn't tear myself away. Almost unconsciously, my hand found its way to my breast and my thumb began stroking my nipple.

Genevieve raised her head and looked straight at Maja.

"I want you to come, cherie. How do you want me to make you come?"

Maja smiled and reached over behind the pillow. She pulled something out and it took me a moment to realize what it was. It was what could only be described as a strapless strap-on dildo, curved on one end to fit inside Genevieve and hit her g-spot and her clitoris, which then continued into a traditional dildo. Maja handed it to Genevieve, who took it, and without taking her eyes of Maja, fit it into place between her own legs. She tossed her hair back and mounted Maja, both woman crying out as she penetrated her.

I must have shifted, or made some noise, because Maja opened her eyes and looked right at me. She smiled and with her finger motioned for me to join them. I must have blushed fifty shades of red as I shook my head no. But my feet were rooted to the spot. I couldn't move. So I continued to stare as Maja pulled Genevieve's head down and whispered in her ear. Both women then turned to look at me, each on the verge of their own ecstasy. I licked my lips. I could practically taste the sex in the air. I could certainly smell it.

Maja closed her eyes, lay her head back on the pillow and, clasping Genevieve's waist with her legs, came violently around her as Genevieve quickly followed. The two of them collapsed against each other, running their hands over each other's bodies. I tore myself away and continued to the bathroom. *Holy shit.*

When I got back to Matt's room I climbed into bed and tried to fall back asleep, but it was no use. I was hot and bothered. I looked over at Matt and lightly traced a line from his ear to his chin, along his jawline. He smiled faintly but otherwise didn't stir. I withdrew my hand and looked up at the ceiling, considering my options.

I could have woken him but then we'd have to talk, and by the time that was done, the mood would have passed. I could've just started touching him—him waking up with his cock in my mouth would certainly have prevented conversation—but I didn't know how that would play out. The easiest thing seemed to be to take matters into my own hands.

I slipped my panties off and reached between my legs, wasting no time as I arched my back to meet my hand. It might've been Maja and Genevieve who'd gotten me going, but at that moment my thoughts were entirely on Matt. I moaned softly and slid my other hand up under my T-shirt, Matt's T-shirt, and started teasing my nipple, rolling it between my fingers, squeezing lightly. I could picture his mouth on mine, his hands skimming over my body.

Suddenly, there was another hand between my legs, and a pair of lips brushing up against my ear.

"Can I help, or am I just meant to watch?" he whispered, his voice thick.

I immediately withdrew both hands and wrapped my arms around his neck, drawing him close.

"Kiss me."

He did, and everything else fell away. The misunderstanding, the anger, the hurt—none of it meant anything as his lips covered mine. It had been so long since he'd kissed me I felt positively light-headed. He pulled away and looked me in the eye, brushing my hair out of my face. I took a deep breath—he smelled delicious. I just wanted to taste him.

I pushed him back on the bed and straddled his hips.

"I have dreamt about you every night since I've been gone," Matt sighed.

"Was I doing anything like this?"

I pushed his shirt up and he obligingly reached up and pulled it off. I leaned over and kissed his neck, running my tongue over the stubbly skin as I closed my eyes. Heaven.

"You might have been doing something like that," he said.

He reached up under my shirt and cupped both my breasts, running his thumbs over my nipples, which hardened under his touch. I made a trail down his chest and stomach, using light kisses and swirling my tongue around his hip bone, ending my journey with a nip. He laughed softly and I looked up at him, gazing into his eyes. I gave him a wicked smile as I lowered his pajama bottoms.

"Hello, there," I whispered as I freed him from his pants.

"You were definitely doing something like that," he sighed.

I got on my knees and took him in my hand, stroking him slowly. He moaned softly, laying his head back on the pillow and running his hands up my thighs. I leaned down and wrapped my mouth around him.

"Allie... that feels amazing. It's been so long..."

He muttered something else, but it was pretty incomprehensible. I smiled around him, catching the fact that he hadn't been with anyone while here. Suddenly, he put his hands under my arms and pulled me back up towards him. I straddled his hips again.

"Hey. I was enjoying that," I said.

"It's almost 4 am, I'm exhausted, and I haven't seen you in almost two months. I want you."

I smiled and started to take off my shirt. He pulled my hands away.

"Leave it. It's sexy, you wearing my shirt."

He rolled me over so I was underneath him, and then he pushed me onto my stomach against the bed. He lowered himself onto me, supporting his weight so as not to crush me. He gathered up my hair, pushing it away from my neck, and leaned down to whisper in my ear.

"I have wanted you since the moment you fainted in my doorway."

He kissed my neck and shoulders, nuzzling me as he went. Using his knee, he pushed my legs apart and I felt a thrill deep in my belly.

"You feel so good. You taste so good. I've missed you, Allie."

I raised my hips off the bed, pushing myself into him, begging him with my body to take me.

"I missed you too, Matt. I came, didn't I?"

He thrust into me and stilled, waiting a breath or two before beginning a steady, almost urgent, rhythm.

"Oh, you will," he whispered in my ear.

I closed my eyes and tried to meet his thrusts, but my position made it impossible for me to do anything but squirm feebly beneath him. I relented and let myself get swept away with him, my body embracing the feel of him inside me, his chest on my back, the warmth of his breath in my ear. I felt him stiffen as he came, and his hands squeezed my shoulders while he bit my neck.

I smiled to myself as he lay still on top of me, trying to regulate his breathing. Slowly, he slid out and rolled on his side, gathering me in towards him, back to chest. He reached around and slid his hand down my belly, between my legs.

"Now," he whispered. "Where were we?"

*

Sometime later, we were lying together on the verge of sleep when Matt kissed the top of my head.

"I'm so glad you're here," he said.

"Me, too."

We lay silent for a moment.

"Matt? Where'd you get the scar?"

He chuckled softly.

"Let's just say I'm living proof that boomerangs work."

"Really? Tell me."

"I was about 13 years old, and my dad came back from a trip to Australia. He brought my sister and me gifts. She got a stuffed koala bear, and I got a boomerang."

"You know, koala bears can be vicious," I said.

He snorted.

"Yeah? Well, her *stuffed* koala was fine. My real boomerang, however, actually came back the first time I threw it and knocked me out, right in my own front yard."

I burst out laughing.

"What the hell was that kiss with Maja?" he asked suddenly.

I stopped laughing and thought about it for a moment.

"I was just curious. I had a pretty tame

college experience."

Matt said nothing. If only he knew what I'd just seen. I closed my eyes and snuggled closer, pulling the blanket up over us.

"Amsterdam is a good place to be curious," he said.

"I'm sure we will have some very interesting adventures."

I looked up at him and he smiled down at me. It was the last thing I remembered before falling asleep.

CHAPTER FOUR

I woke the next morning to an empty bed and a note on the nightstand. *Went to work, didn't want to wake you. I'll take Thursday and Friday off. Text me where you'd like to meet for lunch.* I smiled to myself and rolled over onto my back, staring at the ceiling.

I would spend the morning sightseeing, meet Matt for lunch, and then hit the Van Gogh museum in the afternoon. A little walk afterward and I'd be sure to work up a good appetite for dinner. I had to hit at least seven restaurants over the next five days. I'd made a deal with my editor—she covered my expenses, I turned in a great piece.

I picked up my phone and texted him.

Let's meet at the Rotisserie Amsterdam.
Burgers? You flew all the way here for burgers?
I'm working. You meeting me or not?
Of course I am. 1 pm.

I smiled to myself and got up. I felt compelled to make the bed, something I'd never do at home, but his room was just so neat. It was a shocking revelation to me. I'm not sure why—it just spoke volumes about his personality. Kind, funny, clean—my mother would be thrilled.

I shook off that thought, pulled on a pair of Matt's sweats, and went in search of breakfast. Maja and Genevieve were in the kitchen, in T-shirts and underwear, and I only hesitated for a moment before joining them.

"Good morning," I said, smiling.

They both smiled at me around their toast. I went through the cabinets, and after finding a glass, opened the fridge and pulled out some orange juice.

"There's coffee," Genevieve said.

"Thanks," I said. "I don't actually drink coffee. The only writer I know who doesn't."

"You're a writer?" Genevieve asked.

"Yes. A food critic," I said.

"How very *intéressant*," Genevieve said.

Maja was looking bored with the subject. She turned her attention to me.

"Did you have a good night?" Maja asked with a definite edge of mischief to her voice.

"Very, thank you."

"We're leaving tomorrow, you know. It would be great if you and Matt would come out with us tonight."

"Where are you going?" I asked.

The women looked at each other and grinned.

"We thought we'd catch a show," Maja said.

"Sounds great," I said. "Text me the time and place and we'll meet you there."

CHAPTER FIVE

I walked out of the Rijksmuseum feeling both awed and humbled. I knew it would take more than one visit, so I had planned to do it first thing during my stay. I had only managed to cover a quarter of what I had wanted to see that morning, and I was beginning to realize that a couple of visits could never do that institution justice.

I checked my phone and realized it was already past noon. It was a half-hour walk to the restaurant, so I wasted no time moving through the streets. I was falling in love with the city. It was almost impossible not to. The charming streets, the canals, the tall, narrow buildings, the culture. I was suddenly envious of Matt, that he was able to spend so much time here.

I pulled out my phone again, but this time I dialed Trish. She picked up right away, despite the early hour. I hadn't realized until I heard her sleepy voice that it was only 6:30 in the morning.

"Hey, Allie."

"Trish. I'm so sorry. I didn't realize the time when I called."

"No, no, it's fine. I have to get up in ten minutes anyway. How's it going?"

"Good. Good. How's it going there? Think you can manage until Saturday?"

"Until Saturday? I wish you were gone for months. This is heaven."

"Enjoy. Really. Loki is good?"

"Loki is great. She misses you, but she's just fine. Getting lots of treats."

I laughed.

"Okay. Great. Call me if there's anything."

"Will do. Have fun!"

"Thanks. You, too."

As I approached the restaurant, I was instantly taken in by the red-painted exterior. Then I spotted the handsome guy sitting at one of the two picnic benches parked outside on the makeshift terrace. He was dressed in pants and a dark green button-down that set off his eyes.

Swoon. The table was a long one, meant to be communal, but at the moment he was the only one there.

I slid in and snuggled up against him.

"Hey, there," I said.

"Christ, I could get used to this." Matt said, kissing the top of my head.

I picked up the menu and started reading.

"Is this a working lunch?" he asked.

"Yes," I muttered, giving the menu a final scan.

The waiter approached and smiled at us. Matt looked at me expectantly.

"We'll have Fucking Everything, one of each of the fries, and the Korean fried cauliflower. Matt? Anything else?"

"Uh, no. That should about cover it."

I smiled politely at the waiter and handed him back the menus.

"How many restaurants have you gotta hit?" he asked.

"At least seven in the next five days. I can't eat this heavy all the time, but when they have something called 'Fucking Everything' on the menu, you order it."

Matt laughed. I felt the buzz of a text message in my pocket and reached for my phone. Glancing down, I saw who it was from.

"So Maja and Genevieve are leaving

tomorrow, and they asked if we'd go out with them tonight. To a show," I said.

"A show?"

"Yeah," I said, looking down at my phone. "A place called the Casa Rosso?"

Matt laughed so hard he spat out his water.

"So a sex show, you mean?"

I looked up, shocked and amused at the same time.

"Really? Wow. I'd heard of them but didn't think I'd actually go to one. Have you been?"

Matt shook his head no.

"It'll be interesting, to say the least. How was the Rijksmuseum?"

I smiled, remembering the cool blue walls and the ornate ceiling of the anteroom for the *Night Watch.*

"Amazing. I think I'll spend every morning there. There's just so much to see."

"What did you see this morning?"

I smiled sheepishly.

"The *Night Watch,* of course. I headed straight upstairs. I couldn't resist. And then I got drawn in by all the work in the anteroom and the morning just flew. A week isn't enough."

I stopped short. I didn't want him thinking I was fishing for an invitation to stay longer, so I changed the subject.

"How was your morning? Busy?"

"Kind of. Getting ready for a trip next week."

The waiter arrived with the food, and it was insane. My stomach growled at the sight, and I started salivating at the smell of fried chicken and BBQ ribs. Not to mention that wicked-looking burger in the middle of the plate.

"Holy crap," Matt said. "Do we have to finish it?"

I laughed.

"No. Just enjoy. Where are you going?"

Matt looked up, confused by the question.

"You said you were getting ready for a trip next week. Where are you going?"

"Oh! To Paris. I'm meeting with a client for a bit of consulting. I'm pretty excited. I've never been."

"Me either."

Again I cursed myself. For Christ's sake, I'd shown up on his doorstep completely unannounced. I had no reason to expect him to ask me to stay.

I settled in to eat, and we were silent for the next while as we sampled the different foods. The fries were out of this world, the turbo ones being my favourite. It was a perfect fall day—the sun was shining and there was a crispness to the air, but it was still warm enough not to need a jacket. I looked over at Matt and smiled.

Eventually, I pushed my plate away and sat back.

"I have no idea how you're going to return to work this afternoon. I just want a nap."

Matt laughed. He finished off the rib he was working on, wiped his fingers on a napkin, and sat back with me, kissing the top of my head again. I could get used to that, too.

"What are your plans?"

"I'm going to hit the Van Gogh Museum. What time do you get off?"

"What time is the show?"

"Theatre's open from seven to two. We can show up anytime, stay as long as we want."

Matt rolled his eyes and laughed again.

"Okay. If we're going to do this, let's do it right. Let's meet for an early dinner, then head to the red-light district and hit a sex shop or two. Then we'll meet the women at the theatre. How does that sound?"

"Sounds great to me."

And that's what we did. I spent the afternoon amongst portraits and starry nights, and in the evening, I went to meet Matt for an exquisite dinner at Restaurant Zaza's. Then we found a sex shop.

We walked in and both of us just stood there in stunned silence for about two minutes as we took in our surroundings. It was clean, well-lit, and not at all sleazy looking for a place called Hot Stuff Sex Shop. Very female-friendly.

We started moving through the store, a little shy at first, but warming up to the whole experience as we watched what the other was interested in. We drifted in different directions, each following our own whims. I had clearly piqued his interest with the light bondage because he was looking over a selection of riding crops with a studied focus. I walked up next to him.

I stood there for a moment, surveying the display, then ran my hand lightly over the various models. I stopped at a black one, smiling to myself as I fingered the soft, heart-shaped leather tip.

"I like this one," I whispered.

My hand trailed further along the display, stopping occasionally to inspect an item. There must have been a candle burning somewhere because the entire shop smelled like vanilla and pear. It was erotic, standing there next to him in full public view, selecting the toys we'd later take back to the bedroom.

I stopped at a light brown flogger, with soft, suede-like fringes. I looked over at Matt and raised my eyebrows. He just smiled. I picked it up and, with a flick of my wrist, gave it a test swat against the palm of my hand.

"I wouldn't mind either of those. Or that leather paddle."

Matt's eyebrows flew up and he pulled all three items off the rack.

"Have some expertise in the area, do you?" he asked.

I shrugged and gave him my best coquettish smile.

"Let's just say this ass has been paddled and whipped a few times."

His mouth dropped open.

"You are full of surprises, aren't you?" he asked, amazed.

"Hey. We're in Amsterdam. Why not go wild? I'm up for anything... with you."

He stopped at that and looked me straight in the eye.

"Anything?"

I raised my eyebrows. "What did you have in mind?"

He took in a sharp breath.

"Are you up for anal?"

"Absolutely," I said. "In fact, I saw a nice selection of strap-ons right over there."

I wish I'd pulled out my camera to capture the transformation from hope to pure joy to horrified realization that passed through his eyes in the span of those few seconds. I stifled my laugh, but I couldn't help the smile.

"When you're ready, I'll be ready."

And with that, I walked towards the cash register.

CHAPTER SIX

It was close to eight by the time we got to the theatre. Maja and Genevieve were waiting outside for us, holding hands and giggling at something across the street. We all entered together, and I realized I was completely clueless about what to expect from the evening. Ever the researcher, I had somehow neglected to even find out what goes on at one of these things.

The theatre itself was surprisingly nice. Cushioned seats in the performance area, with a full bar and a lounge with comfy chairs beside it. We found our place and settled in as a couple was having sex on stage. I shouldn't have been shocked. I was at a sex show. What followed, in no particular order, were strippers, more live sex, women with some interesting props, some light S&M (through which I kept a close eye on Matt's face) and then a closing act that, unfortunately, would never allow me to look at a banana in the same way again.

It was a strange experience. Mildly erotic at times, but mainly just a curiosity. That didn't seem to stop our dates, however, as they made out passionately through the entire show. Matt and I were at times a little embarrassed, a little uneasy, a little amused, and maybe just a little turned on. It was a confusing evening.

After the first run-through of the entire performance, I realized it would just be the same acts repeating over and over until closing. I also knew Matt had to work the next morning.

"Want to go?" I whispered.

"Yes."

I looked over at Maja and tugged the back of her shirt to get her attention. She pulled herself away from Genevieve and looked at me quizzically.

"What's wrong?"

"Nothing's wrong. Matt and I are leaving."

"Leaving? Why?"

"Well, we've seen the show, so we're ready to go. You stay."

The girls looked at each other and then looked at me.

"We were kind of hoping the two of you would join the two of us..."

I felt Matt stiffen beside me. I had no idea what was going through his head, but I turned back to Maja and smiled politely.

"You thought this was foreplay?" I asked.

Maja shrugged, smiling.

"That's an intriguing offer, but I think we'll pass. If I don't see you in the morning, I hope you enjoy the rest of your travels."

I leaned over and kissed her lightly on the mouth, knowing she'd get a kick out of it. She pulled me closer, refusing to let me out of her grip. I laughed against her mouth until she gave in and let go, laughing at herself in defeat.

"One of these days..." she said wistfully.

*

The flat felt empty with Maja and Genevieve's departure. We made the most of our time alone together, with an unspoken goal of christening every surface in the place. Sex in Maja's bed had been particularly hot as I recalled the scene I'd witnessed only days earlier. I came three times that evening, each orgasm stronger than the last. Matt felt like a fucking king.

I spent my mornings at the Rijksmuseum, exploring the different collections and discovering new artists. I stood mesmerized for close to an hour one day in front of the *Night School* by Gerard Dou, a work clearly influenced by Rembrandt. The play of light and dark was breathtaking, and I couldn't tear myself away. In the afternoons I visited Anne Frank's House, a few cafes, and I hit a few other museums. But I kept returning to my first love, the Rijksmuseum. I wished I had more time.

Matt and I met for lunch and dinner every day. He humoured me even when I picked the tourist traps. I spent time in the late afternoons or early mornings writing either the food column or the erotica. I still hadn't told Matt about the latter. I didn't know how to bring it up, or how he'd take it. Besides, I reasoned he'd never have to find out. Everything was anonymous. The only living souls who knew I was writing that column were my editor, Lynn, and myself.

On Thursday evening, when I met Matt for dinner, he was grinning from ear to ear like he had some huge secret he wasn't sure he should share with me.

"Spill it," I said, sliding into the bench across from him.

"You're not sitting next to me tonight?"

I started for a moment. Had he really just noticed something that small? It was true. I had been sitting next to him each night. What made me sit across from him? If Lynn were here, she'd have said I was slowly pulling away in anticipation of my departure in three days. I sighed, forced to admit imaginary Lynn was right. Still, I didn't move.

"I want to stare at your pretty face," I said, smiling.

"I like it when I can touch you," he said.

I reached my hand across the table in concession, and as he took it I felt that familiar sensation pass through my body; the same one that set fire to my veins every time we touched. When we first met, I had assumed it was just chemistry. Pure lust. That this would be a fun little adventure and it would fizzle out. But the closer I got to leaving, the more I was dreading it. The more I worried I was falling for him. And when he made these little remarks, observations, gestures… it made me wonder if he was falling for me, too.

He kissed my knuckles and when the waiter arrived, he pleasantly surprised me by ordering the entire dinner.

"I've been paying attention," he said. "I like taking an interest in your work."

"So why don't we ever talk about your work?" I asked.

"My work is boring. Besides," he said, changing the subject, "I have a surprise for you."

"Hmm. I don't always like surprises."

"You'll like this one," he said.

He smiled that same smile he was wearing when I showed up, and I couldn't help but play along.

"Okay, what is it?"

"Well, you know how that guy, Greg, is showing up tonight?"

My heart fell. We hadn't even gotten to the kitchen yet. I had really wanted to take that countertop for a spin.

"Yeah. That's no surprise."

"Well, I was kind of enjoying our privacy, and seeing as how you're leaving in a few days, I rented us a houseboat."

I may have squealed.

"A houseboat!"

If possible, Matt smiled even wider. There was sheer pleasure on his face at having delighted me. I scaled back my reaction. This could not end well.

"Matt. That was really sweet. Unnecessary, but sweet. Where is it?"

"We'll pick up some clothes and… things…

after dinner and walk over. It's not far from the flat."

I slipped off my shoe and ran my foot up his leg under the table, resting it on the bench between his legs. He squeezed his legs shut and I laughed, wiggling my toes to show him the advantage he just gave me. His legs immediately snapped open again. The poor guy. I knew I was torturing him, but I just couldn't stop.

"You're playing dangerous games with me?"

"Not at all. Pay attention, the food's here."

For the rest of the meal, every time he attempted to take a bite of his dinner, I'd casually shift my foot. His face may have displayed frustration, but the movement in his pants told me a different story.

"You are trouble, you know that?"

"Don't you forget it."

We spent the rest of the meal flirting outrageously with each other as my toes wreaked havoc on his most tender of parts. By the time dessert was over, he was practically panting. I signed for the bill and looked over at him, cool as a cucumber.

"Want to catch a movie? Maybe walk over to the Leidseplein?"

"Are you kidding me right now? I want to bend you over this table and fuck your brains out. We're going straight back to the apartment, I'm going to take you very quickly, very roughly in the bedroom, and then we're going to pack up and head to the houseboat. I haven't yet decided what to do with you once we get there."

Now I was panting, too.

"Roughly?"

"You have been purposefully torturing me throughout this entire meal. There is no way you're coming that first time. That will be for my pleasure."

Granted, we hadn't been together longer than eight days in total, but I'd never seen this side of Matt before. I mean, he was amazing in bed, but taking the lead in this way? He who had never spanked a woman being devious enough to deny my pleasure as a form of sexual revenge? My pleasure always came first with Matt. I should've been appalled, but I'd never been more turned on in my life.

CHAPTER SEVEN

We stumbled into the apartment, barely able to keep our hands off each other until we came face-to-face with Greg. He was standing in the middle of the living room and was simply the most gorgeous creature I'd ever seen before in real life. Probably in his late twenties, he was a Greek god personified—golden blond locks, blue eyes, muscles on top of muscles. I was licking my lips before I could stop myself.

"You must be Matt," he said, approaching us.

"Yeah. Greg?"

"That's me."

"Nice to meet you, man. This is my...uh... friend, Allie."

I smiled and put out my hand, anxious for this hunk of a man to touch me, even briefly. He took my hand and shook it firmly.

"Nice to meet you, Allie."

I smiled, completely incapable of speech.

"Actually, Greg, you've got the place to yourself for a couple of nights. Allie and I just came to collect some stuff and we'll, or I'll, be back on Saturday."

Greg raised his eyebrows in surprise.

"Oh. Okay. I'll see you then."

He fell back onto the couch and flipped on the TV, but his eyes didn't leave us until we were safely inside Matt's room, door locked.

"You like that, do you?" Matt asked, laughing softly.

"Come on, he was gorgeous."

"Lucky I'm not the jealous type."

Matt came at me and grabbed the hem of my shirt. Putting his arm around my waist, he pulled me close to him, my back to his chest. He walked me over to the dresser and reached down to undo his pants. As they fell to his ankles, he pushed up my skirt and pulled down my underwear.

"In a rush, are you?" I asked.

"Hell, yes."

"Greg is right outside this door."

"I give zero fucks."

He ran his hands up the front of my body, grabbing my breasts with more force than usual for him. He bent his head, gently biting and kissing my neck while pressing his hips into me, so I could feel him grow hard.

"Remember," he whispered. "This is not for you."

He removed one of his hands from my breast and reach down between my legs. There was little for him to do—I was more than ready. I grabbed onto the dresser as he thrust into me, then repeated the motion again and again, one hand on my hip and the other squeezing my breast.

The room spun away from me. I held tighter to the dresser, trying to stay silent. His clear, desperate need for me was so overwhelming it was intoxicating. He came within ten strokes and I heard him groan in my ear as he collapsed against my back. I gave him a moment to recover, the gently pulled him out of me and turned to face him.

"You don't like when I tease you?" I asked.

He studied me for a moment as if deciding whether to speak.

"I like that you give me an excuse to be rough. I've never done that before, and I won't lie, it's a turn-on."

I stepped out of my panties and pulled my

skirt down, straightening it. I walked over the night table and opened the drawer, pulling out our small collection of toys and dropping them into a backpack. I put the bag down on the bed and walked over to him, wrapping my arms around his neck.

"I think we're going to have a very good time tonight," I whispered in his ear.

His lips found mine and he kissed me, long and deep. My nipples hardened against his chest, straining at the fabric of my dress. He grabbed my waist and pulled me towards him. I could have stayed there forever, never coming up for air. I had never sexually connected with anyone like this before. Two more days.

Matt pulled away, looking at me, eyes filled with lust.

"Let's go," he said, his voice husky.

*

We walked through the cool evening air until Matt led me down one street that ran along a canal. There were houseboats all along the quay and they were just beautiful, strung lights twinkling in the moonlight. The air smelled of fall and the distinct scent of the canal. It was absolutely romantic, and I couldn't help but take Matt's hand. He looked over at me, surprised. I gave him a quick squeeze, then let go. I kept forgetting myself. This was fun. This was not love. I was leaving in two days.

Matt stopped outside a beautiful, blue-painted houseboat. It was small in comparison to the others, but the deck wrapped around the entire boat and it was lined with lush green plants and flowers. We walked the short plank to the front door and Matt fit the key into the lock. I could barely contain my smile as he opened the door and we walked inside.

The only word to describe it was charming. A cozy living room, an ample dining area, and a decent-sized kitchen greeted us as soon as we entered. The bedroom was towards the back, and it contained a master bathroom with a shower big enough for the two of us. We burst out laughing, positively giddy.

The bedroom itself wasn't huge, but it was certainly spacious enough. It held a queen-sized bed made up with thick duvets and fluffy pillows. Four posts of painted white carved wood sprang up at each corner of the bed, giving the entire room an elegant feel. The dresser was also wood and painted white, distressed to match. I flopped down on the bed, delighted with our accommodations. I reached over and lit the candle on the bedside table. Matt looked at me, hunger in his eyes.

"Get up," he said.

I stood.

"Take off your clothes."

I did.

"Lie down. On your back."

I climbed onto the bed and crawled towards the headboard.

Matt walked over to his bag and pulled out four neckties. *My, oh my.* He'd put some thought into this evening. I suddenly wondered if he'd chosen this particular boat for the bed but couldn't bring myself to ask.

"You're going to be a good girl, aren't you?"

He started tying up one of my wrists and securing it to the post.

"Depends. What happens if I'm bad?"

"Even better," he said, as he continued to secure my other wrist.

He smiled at his handiwork and moved down to the end of the bed, where he took each of my calves in turn, gently securing my ankles and then tying them to their corresponding posts. I was left spread-eagled, entirely vulnerable, and completely on fire.

Matt stood and took a deep breath as he looked at me. The look in his eyes told me that even though I was the one tied up, I was also the one with all the power. It was a heady sensation, and I felt sexy as fuck.

"You look beautiful," he said, stepping away.

"Where are you going?" I asked, suddenly worried.

"Well, here's what I was thinking. I was going to leave you here for a bit, you know, to get all squirmy like you do, while I go out onto the deck and smoke a joint."

"You're going to what now?" I asked in disbelief.

"You heard me."

He was being awfully glib. But despite what I thought of him at that moment, his tactics were sound. I was already wet and doing my damnedest not to squirm.

"And how long do you intend to be gone?" I asked, trying to sound nonchalant.

"Not sure. But if you've had enough, just say purple banana."

"Oh," I said, blinking at him. "Are we into safe words now?"

"You know, you're kind of taking the fun out of all of this."

I nodded at him.

"Okay, fine. Go. Smoke. I'll be here. Waiting for you."

I arched my back a little, just to show him I was okay with all this. I smiled and wiggled my hips.

"Or, you can just stay here," I said as seductively as I could muster.

He raised his eyebrows, smiled, and walked out. He left the door open so I could see him settle on the couch. He reached into his bag and pulled out a small tin. He rolled himself a joint, all the while humming to himself under his breath. When he was done, he stood up and opened the back door of the houseboat, directly onto the deck that overlooked the canal.

Fuck. He learned quick. As soon as he exited onto the deck, I lost sight of him. I had no watch, no way to tell the time. I lay there, staring up at the ceiling for god knows how long. As my initial irritation faded—maybe I would've liked a little doobie, too—the original sense of arousal returned. I closed my eyes and felt the heat spread between my legs. I ached to touch myself but was bound to the bed. It was torture. I couldn't keep my hips still. I took a deep breath. I could smell him. Probably from the neckties that held my wrists.

And then I felt it. The first flick of the crop. I opened my eyes, and there he was, standing right over me, wicked smile on his lips and pure desire in his gaze. I moaned and arched my back as the leather hit my nipple. He stopped, letting the tip graze along my skin down towards my belly, my thighs. Chills followed in the crop's wake, raising goosebumps as it went. My head was swimming but the rest of my body was at attention, awaiting the next strike.

I let out a soft moan and he raised his wrist, catching me once more, across the tender flesh on the inside of my thigh.

"Matt..."

"Allie..."

He threw the crop to the ground and fell onto the bed. He took my face in his hands and kissed me, his tongue searching, asking, seeking, and eventually finding what it was looking for as I kissed him back, giving him everything I had.

His lips left mine and trailed down my neck, kissing, licking, teasing his way down towards my breasts. He took my nipple in his mouth, gently sucking and biting, forcing cries from deep within me. But he was too impatient even then. He kept moving downward until he was firmly between my legs, tongue deep inside me, palms pressed against my inner thighs.

I came fast and I came hard. Being unable to shut my legs, the orgasm carried on longer than I would have let it, and it coursed through my body in wracking waves, over and over again. I longed to wrap my fingers in his hair, my legs around his neck. I cried out again, and this time he showed me mercy, gently moving away, giving me a final kiss between the legs before bringing himself up to untie my wrists. I immediately pulled his head down towards me again and kissed him. He indulged me for a moment, then moved down to untie my ankles.

"Allie..."

"Come back," I whispered.

He climbed on top of me again and slowly slid inside, and together we moved, slowly at first and then faster, faster until he raised himself on his hands and thrust into me one last time, grunting as he came. He collapsed on top of me and I stroked his hair.

"You know, you could take your time a little, with the crop."

"No, I can't. Christ, I get so turned on I want you right away."

Matt laughed at himself.

"I'm sorry. I guess it's still new. I'm a failure at kink."

I lifted my head to kiss him gently on the mouth.

"You are no failure."

I rolled over and he pulled me towards him, kissing the top of my head. I wished he'd stop doing that. I was growing to love it. We still hadn't discussed my departure, what would happen. I guess neither of us wanted to spoil the mood; the illusion that this was our life.

I fell asleep wondering when we'd get around to it. Less than forty-eight hours to my flight.

CHAPTER EIGHT

I woke up early Friday morning. Matt was still fast asleep, so I crept out of bed and slipped on his T-shirt. I tip-toed out of the bedroom and searched for my bag. Finding it, I extracted my laptop and headed for the deck, grabbing a blanket off the couch on my way out the door.

I settled into one of the comfy deck chairs and wrapped the blanket around me. It was a chilly October morning, though it held the promise of a beautiful sunny day. I settled the computer onto my lap, opened it up, and pulled up a fresh document. With a smile on my face, I started typing up our adventures of the night before. I was cutting it close in submitting my column and I was terrified of pissing off my new editor. This gig was the chance of a lifetime—all I had to do was come up with the material.

I'd certainly collected enough over the past week, but that wasn't the reason I'd come. Now I wondered if I had made a mistake. He seemed to be enjoying my company, but he also made no move to encourage me to stay. I put it all out of my head as I returned to my piece.

I was hard at work, oblivious to my surroundings, and didn't even hear Matt come up behind me. When his hand hit my shoulder, I jumped and screamed. He just laughed.

"You scare easy," he said.

"I do. Always have. And faint. As you know."

I smiled, embarrassed.

"What are you working on? Food column?" he asked.

I closed the top of my computer and put it aside, turning to face him.

"No. Something different."

"Different? Why didn't you tell me? What are you working on?"

I wanted to tell him. I really, really did. But for some reason, I couldn't. Maybe it was for the same reason we hadn't discussed my impending departure or the future of whatever we were doing.

"It's a surprise," I said. "Come, kiss me."

*

Matt and I ordered in three meals that day, neither of us wanting to waste one precious moment of that houseboat. We both agreed it was the best. There was just something about being right on the water. We lazed around all day, making out, having sex. I even gave up my precious last trip to the Rijksmuseum.

After dinner, though, Matt looked at me with a funny look in his eye.

"What is it?" I asked.

"I thought maybe we'd go out for a bit," he said with a slight hesitancy in his voice.

"What did you have in mind?"

"Well, given it's your last night in Amsterdam, I thought maybe we'd walk back down to the red-light district and take in a peep show."

I raised my eyebrow at him.

"Well, well."

"I'm curious, and it's certainly not something I'll do alone. You said you're up for anything."

He was right. I grabbed my sweater.

"Let's go."

We walked through the dark streets of

Amsterdam, side by side, a little nervous but buzzing with a strange sense of excitement. Yes, we'd seen people having sex at the Casa Rosso, but this somehow seemed more intimate, despite the fact there would be glass separating us. And given the amount of sex we'd already had that day, I figured I'd be able to enjoy this without the need to rush out of there and fuck Matt's brains out. It might make for good column material.

Once we hit the red-light district, we drifted along, stopping occasionally to watch the women behind the windows selling their wares. Despite the touristy nature of the whole thing, I couldn't deny I was starting to get a little hot. I didn't know if it was because of the prostitutes touching themselves, or the thought of what we were about to witness.

"Let's party first," I said to Matt.

He smiled in relief and took my elbow. We found a nearby coffee shop and ducked inside. Settling into the red upholstered chairs by the wall, we gave our order and waited.

"You nervous?" he asked.

"No," I lied.

The waiter returned and Matt lit the joint. He took a long drag, then passed it to me. I accepted it gratefully.

"Allie..."

"Yes?"

"Come to Paris with me next week."

I coughed, almost dropping the joint. He sat up straight and passed me one of the two glasses of water on the table in front of us. He looked almost panicked.

"Look, we said nothing serious. I'm not asking you for that. I'm just asking you to extend your trip a couple of days and join me in Paris. It would be so much fun. We could eat cheese and bread and fuck in French."

I broke out into a huge smile.

"I would love to go to Paris with you."

"You would?"

He seemed genuinely relieved. What girl wouldn't go to Paris with him? Paris! Of course I would go.

"Don't you have to check in with work, or with Trish?" he asked.

"I spoke to Trish earlier this week. She practically begged me to stay longer. And don't worry about work. I've got it covered."

I could write smut from anywhere, as long as I filed my story on time. We finished the joint, a renewed energy between us. He'd made it perfectly clear—this was just for fun. I could do fun. At least the boundaries were clear. He stood and reached over to help me up.

We exited the coffee shop and walked up the

street. Once again we found ourselves standing outside the Casa Rosso, the only establishment left in Amsterdam with a running peep show.

"Ready?" he asked.

"Ready."

We walked in and were led to a small private booth with a bench and a glass partition, behind which was a curtain. We were instructed it was two euros a minute and left alone. We looked at each other and then around the tiny space. At least it was clean.

We sat down, side by side, and Matt leaned forward to slip in the two euros. The curtains opened, revealing two people, a man and a woman, having some very explicit sex, awfully close up. We both gasped as our brains registered what we were witnessing. We stared, silent, enrapt, until the curtain closed and Matt leaned forward with more money.

We watched them for at least five minutes, going through various positions while touching and kissing each other, completely oblivious to our presence. I was starting to squirm, incredibly turned on despite myself. Matt noticed and handed me his fistful of euros.

"What are you doing?" I asked.

He said nothing as he slid to the floor and knelt in front of me, lifting my skirt and pushing aside my panties. I sighed as his tongue lightly touched the tip of my clitoris, sending waves echoing throughout my body. As the curtain closed, I leaned forward with the coins, pushing myself into Matt at the same time.

He grabbed my ass and brought me in closer, invading every part of me with his tongue. I writhed on the bench, transfixed by the couple before me having sex, and the sheer brazen gall of Matt to be on his knees before me in a public place. I clutched his hair but as his tongue worked harder, I cried out and pressed my palms flat against the sides of our booth. I raised myself off the bench, wanting him further inside me. His fingers dug into my ass, making me cry again, completely uncaring of who might hear me.

As the woman in front of me erupted into orgasm underneath the man impaling her from behind, I came fiercely beneath Matt's tongue. It was the dirtiest, filthiest, most erotic thing I'd ever done. I couldn't catch my breath. Matt stood up and grabbed my hand.

"Let's go. I have to get you home."

CHAPTER NINE

A few days later, when I should have been recovering from monster jetlag, Matt and I were traipsing through the streets of Paris. We had the best time in the city built for lovers. We spent hours in cafes, drinking and people-watching. I managed to convince Sarah to let me do a piece on Paris dives, and we had a blast eating the greasiest food we could find.

"You're going to kill me," Matt said on the second evening.

"Oh, come on. You're made of tougher stuff than that."

I laughed at him and reached for another French fry, dipping it in aioli and bringing it up to his lips. He groaned in protest, but opened his mouth nonetheless. He closed his eyes as he ate. Then he opened them and looked straight at me.

"I just can't resist."

Seeing the look on my face, he stopped short.

"What? What's wrong?"

"Nothing," I said. "What were you going to say?"

"French fries. I can't resist French fries. Especially these."

I smiled, but inside I exhaled in relief. For an insane moment I had thought he was going to say he couldn't resist me. I'd been treading a careful line the past few days. The kisses on top of my head, the casual expressions of affection —I was definitely growing fond of those. But once again, in a few days I'd be gone.

We finished our meal and took a stroll down the left bank of the Seine. We passed Notre Dame, still closed after the fire. We stood there for a few minutes, trying to take in the enormity of it all.

"What will you do tomorrow?" Matt asked.

"The Louvre, probably. Or the Jus de Paume. I hit the Louvre this morning, but I'd love to go back there before we leave."

"I can't believe it's already Wednesday. We leave Friday morning. I should've booked through the weekend. That was so dumb. I guess I just figured you'd want to get back."

I snorted. Matt looked at me.

"What?"

"Yes, please. I'd much rather get back to my shitty apartment than stare out at the Notre Dame Cathedral, whatever its current status. Are you crazy?"

Matt tilted his head as he considered me but didn't speak for a moment. He looked back out over the water and without turning back, spoke very quietly.

"Would you consider staying longer?"

My heart stopped. No matter what I did, I could not prevent the smile that spread across my lips. I tried to steady my breathing before I spoke.

"In Paris?"

Matt was silent again.

"No. I mean a few more weeks in Europe. In Amsterdam."

I didn't say anything for the longest time. This was what I had dreamed about, what I had wished for. But at the same time, I was terrified of what it meant. Of what it would mean to Matt. More than anything, I wanted to call Lynn. I looked at Matt, who wore the most expectant look on his face. My heart went out to him. Then I checked myself.

"Let me think about it. Can I let you know

when we get back to Amsterdam?"

He smiled, clearly unsure of what that meant. I moved closer to him, standing behind him and sliding my hands around to his front, clasping them just over the button on his jeans. I put my chin on his shoulder and stared out at the water. I kissed his neck, his ear, and got up on my toes to nuzzle that soft spot just at the base where his neck meets his shoulder.

"Isn't it gorgeous?" I said.

He grunted in reply. I looked around. We were completely alone. It was late and the streets were deserted. I deftly undid the button on his jeans and slipped my hand inside. He put his hand on mine to stop me, but I wrested it free.

"Shhh…" I whispered in his ear.

"Allie."

"No one is here. No one can see."

I slid my hand in further, until I found him. At least part of him was ready to play. I smiled against his neck as I began to stroke him against the confines of his jeans.

"Imagine if it were my mouth," I whispered.

He groaned as I wrapped my hand tighter around him. I moved in closer against him, breasts pressing into his back, lips brushing his ear. I felt a rush between my legs as he slowly succumbed to my will.

"Imagine if I were down on my knees, right here on the streets of Paris, with your cock in my mouth."

I moved my hand faster, grinding up against him from behind as I worked. He moaned softly.

"I love when I can wrap my lips around you, let my tongue explore… when you get so hard I can graze you with my teeth and drive you over the edge…"

"Oh, god, Allie…"

It took no time at all for him to come, right there, leaning up against the low barrier along the Seine on a beautiful fall night in Paris. He removed my hand from his pants, zipped up, and turned to look at me.

"You are the hottest fuck I've ever had."

I smiled.

"I will take that as a compliment."

I turned on my heel to walk away and came face to face with an elderly couple in their mid-70s. They were looking straight at us, clearly aware of what we'd just done. But there was zero judgment in their eyes. In fact, they smiled at me and carried on.

Ah, the French.

Matt caught up to me and together we walked back to the hotel. Of the male species, and having just orgasmed, he fell asleep immediately upon dropping down onto the bed. I suppressed a smile and took the opportunity to pull out my laptop. So far, Paris had provided us with many adventures such as we'd had tonight, and I hadn't had the time to write about them yet. I settled in for a few hours of work, content to look over at Matt every once in a while, watching as he slept.

CHAPTER TEN

It was just before noon on Friday morning when we arrived back at the flat in Amsterdam. We walked into the apartment to find Greg zipping up a weekend bag on the coffee table.

"Hey," Matt said. "Off somewhere?"

Greg smiled at us, giving us that thousand-watt flash of teeth.

"I'm off to Ibiza for the weekend. I'll be back Sunday night. Have fun in Paris?"

"It was lovely, thank you," I said.

And with that, Greg blew us both kisses and was out the door. Matt and I looked at each other and smiled.

"Alone again," Matt purred. "Luck follows

us."

He started towards me and I put out my hand to stop him.

"Before you get any ideas, I have errands to run. Including picking up some lunch. You stay here, I'll be back soon."

"One little kiss," he said.

I shook my head.

"I'm all too familiar with your 'little kisses.' Just wait."

Matt dropped down on the couch.

"Yes, ma'am," he said.

I walked through the neighbourhood streets, looking for any restaurant that caught my fancy. Truth was, I had no errands. I just needed the time to think about Matt's offer. Should I stay? For how long? I was having the time of my life, and I didn't want to ruin that by overstaying my welcome or trying to turn this into something it was not. Matt was clear — this was just for fun. This did not change the terms of our…whatever it was.

I pulled out my phone and checked the time. One o'clock. A respectable seven a.m. back home. I called Trish. She picked up right away.

"Allie! You staying longer?"

I burst out laughing.

"I'd like to."

"Please, please, please do."

"You make it very easy, Trish."

"It's just been perfect. Really. I'm happy. Loki's happy. I assume you're getting laid. Stay!"

"I might just do that."

"Yay!!"

I hung up the phone, smiling. My smile faded as I dialed Sarah. I wasn't sure she'd be as forgiving.

"What do you mean you're not coming back?" she asked. "Ever?"

"Of course I'm coming back. Matt's only here for another four months, so that's the longest I'd be. But I may only stay a few weeks."

There was a pause on the line, and my heart sunk.

"I need a restaurant critic, Allie. Not a galloping gourmet."

"I know."

"Will you take a leave without pay?"

I thought about it. I still had the erotica.

"I think I would. You'd replace me?"

"Just temporarily. Unless you decide otherwise. You've always got a job here, Allie."

"Thanks, Sarah."

I hung up the phone. That was two out of three. I took a deep breath and dialed again.

"Tara Sheen."

My erotica editor terrified me. I had never even met her in person, but I imagined she must be at least six feet tall. I felt like I was back in grade school whenever I spoke to her.

"Hi, Tara, it's Allie."

"Allie. How are you?"

"I'm great."

"Still in Europe?"

"Actually, yes. I was thinking of staying a while longer."

"I read the stuff you sent me yesterday. Will I get more of that if you stay?"

I had her.

"That's the plan."

"Enjoy yourself, then."

There was a momentary silence. I didn't speak, sensing she wanted to say something more.

"Your column is doing very well, Allie. Temple Fraser has become a star of the website. I'm surprised you haven't heard anything there yet."

I stopped dead in my tracks.

"What?"

"You heard me. Good job."

And she hung up. Just like that. What did she mean? A star? How well? They'd only run three columns so far. Damn, that woman was infuriating. But I had no time to be upset because suddenly I realized I had one more call to make. I looked at my phone and reluctantly dialed.

"Allie Styles. How the hell have you been?"

"Hi, Lynn."

"Why haven't you called? When did you get back?"

"I'm not back. I'm still here."

Silence.

"Lynn?"

"What's going on, Allie?"

"We were having fun, so he asked me to go with him to Paris. He was going for work. We had a great time, and he asked me to stay a few weeks longer. I think I might."

More silence.

"And how do you feel about him?"

"I like him. That's all. We're having a great time. He's a great guy."

"He is. Do you think there could be more? I've never known you to fly across an ocean for fun."

Now it was my turn to be silent.

"I don't know, Lynn. Maybe that's why I want to stay. I've been telling myself this is just for fun, but if he's open to it, I might be open to it. And we'll only find out if I'm here."

"That actually makes sense."

I smiled to myself. We said our goodbyes,

hung up, and I continued on my walk. With all of that off my chest, it dawned on me that I'd done it. I could stay with a paycheck and a clear conscience. I could, for the first time since Josh, try to forge a relationship with a decent guy.

I decided right there that I would go back to the flat and tell him, and finally have the relationship conversation. It had been long enough. If I was in for the long haul, it was time to talk commitment. Excited, I picked up my pace and moved with a purpose, finding a restaurant within the next half block.

By the time I got back to the flat, I was positively humming. I couldn't wait to tell Matt. Holding onto the takeout bag, I pushed open the door with my hip and saw him sitting on the couch, reading something off his phone.

I gave him a huge smile and walked towards him.

"I have great news."

"Hold on," he said.

He never even lifted his eyes from his phone. He sat, with his hand poised midair, as he finished reading whatever had so captured his attention. I put down the bag on the table and sat beside him on the couch. He tilted his phone slightly, so it was just out of my view. I shrugged and leaned back.

Finally, he put down his phone and, without looking at me, asked, "Does the name Temple Fraser mean anything to you?"

Oh, shit.

"Let me guess," he said. "You were going to tell me. You just hadn't found the right time."

His tone was cold and dripping with accusation. I shrunk back into my seat.

"Allie. This is us."

"But no one knows it's us," I offered meekly.

"That's not the point. You should have discussed this with me."

At first, I thought he'd sounded angry. Then I realized he was just hurt. It was like a knife through my heart.

"I know. You're right. I actually wrote the first piece for you, but I was embarrassed to show it to you. And then I showed it to my editor, and she referred me to another editor, and before I knew it I was being paid a lot of money to write more."

Matt started and looked at me. I couldn't read his expression, but I knew it wasn't good.

"Is that why you're here? For material?"

"No! I came because I wanted to see you," I cried.

The material was secondary, but I figured it was best to leave that part out.

"And I decided to stay. That's what I was

coming to tell you."

Matt stood up and started pacing. My heart sank. He'd changed his mind. There was a knock at the door. We looked at each other and Matt walked over to answer it. He opened the door and there stood Maja, grinning from ear to ear.

"Matt! Allie! I'm so happy to see you!"

"Maja," Matt said. "What are you doing here?"

"I'm off to Ibiza in the morning and thought I'd see if my room was vacant. You know, on the down-low."

She smiled that Maja smile.

"Maja, it's really not a good time."

I stood up and walked over to the door.

"Actually, Maja, it is free. Greg just left for Ibiza this morning. What an interesting coincidence. Come, I'll get you some fresh sheets."

And with that, I took Maja's hand, led her into the second bedroom, and shut the door.

CHAPTER ELEVEN

I sat down on the bed and looked at Maja. I had no clue what she saw in my eyes.

"Am I about to get lucky?" she asked.

I burst into tears.

"I guess not."

She came over and sat next to me on the bed. She put an arm around me, and I put my head on her shoulder, welcoming the comfort.

"What happened?"

"Matt and I had a fight."

"You're kidding," she said, sarcasm dripping from each word.

I laughed and wiped my eyes.

"He'll get over it," she insisted.

"I was wrong."

Maja didn't say anything for a while.

"What did you do?" she asked.

"I wrote about him."

Maja looked at me.

"Anonymously," I added quickly.

"Did you paint him in a bad light?" she asked, hesitant.

"No! Not at all."

"He'll get over it."

She stood and moved her bag onto the bed, unzipping it and pulling out a camisole. She started taking off her clothes, walking around the room and inspecting the changes Greg had made as she did so. She turned to me, fully naked.

"What's he like, this Greg?"

I laughed.

"He's gorgeous. Looks like a Greek god."

She pulled on her camisole and a pair of underwear and climbed onto the bed. She pulled back the covers and slid in.

"You staying with me tonight?"

"You didn't even change the sheets."

Maja shrugged.

"I like Greek gods. You staying?"

"Would that be okay?"

Maja smiled and patted the mattress next to her.

"Maja…"

"I know, I know. I'm just kidding. Of course you can stay. I won't touch. Promise."

I pulled off my jeans and my bra and slid under the covers next to her. She put an arm around me, pulling me in close, chest to back. She whispered in my ear.

"Don't worry. Everything is going to be fine. You'll see."

As I drifted off to sleep, I prayed she was right.

*

I woke up sometime in the middle of the night and found Matt crouching down by the side of the bed, my hand in his. His eyes were pleading.

"Allie, come to bed."

I disentangled myself from Maja's limbs and followed him sleepily through the flat and into his bedroom. I crawled under the covers and closed my eyes. Matt crawled in after me, taking my face in his hands and peppering my face with tiny kisses.

"I'm sorry, Allie. Really."

"It's okay, Matt," I murmured. "We'll talk about it in the morning."

"It's not okay. I'm an ass. Let me make up for it."

That woke me a little.

"What did you have in mind?"

He continued his trail of kisses along my jawbone, arriving at my mouth. He put his hand under my chin as he kissed me so lightly it may have been a dream. He continued down my neck, pulling aside my V-neck to kiss the tops of my breasts. I felt each individual hair on my body stand on end.

I moaned despite myself. Taking it as encouragement, Matt lifted my shirt, pulling it off over my head. He ran his hands down my body, using his mouth to kiss, lick, and suck as he worked his way down. Thoughts of our earlier argument melted away as my mind filled with pure sensation. I was completely his, and he knew it.

He pulled down my underwear, pausing only briefly to nuzzle between my legs. Then he stood up, pulled off his own underwear, and grabbing my ankles, pulled me to the edge of the bed.

He flipped me over and pulled me further down, so I was bent over the side of the mattress. Standing behind me, he took hold of my hips as he entered me, working himself in slowly. I pushed back to meet him, anticipating each thrust. He increased his speed and I gripped the sheets above my head.

Suddenly, he stilled. I raised my hips, encouraging him to move, but he wouldn't.

"Matt…"

Slowly, he began to move again, and as he did, he gave my ass a quick slap. I cried out in surprise. He moved faster, gripping my hips once again, driving himself into me.

"Oh, yes, Matt…"

Without mercy, he slammed into me, over and over. I reached down between my legs and rubbed myself, aching to join him when he found his release. I moved beneath him, forcing him to quicken his pace even more. I came violently, loudly, as he continued to thrust. I reached down further, grabbing his balls and squeezing until I felt them constrict on their own as he reached his own climax, digging his fingers into my hips.

When we were done, I crawled back onto the bed and under the covers. I pulled them up to my chin and studied him as he searched for his underwear before coming to join me. I lay there, waiting for my pulse to return to normal. The sex had been awesome, but a little unusual for him. My always-do-right, consent-is-best guy just engaged in rough make-up sex, whereas I'd thought he'd be more of the gentle caresses sort.

Odd, but not necessarily bad, I thought, as I

drifted off to sleep.

*

"So how does it work?" Matt asked.

It was later the next morning and we were sitting on the terrace of a café by the canal. It was a beautiful day, but we were the only ones sitting outside. Such tourists. I was peeling the layers off my Danish as I waited for my tea to cool.

"The column?"

"Yeah."

"Well, I write, and my editor pays me."

"Enough?"

I smiled at him.

"Enough that I'm here."

He smiled back.

"Then I guess I should just shut up and be grateful," he said quietly.

He reached across the table and took my hand, staring deep into my eyes. No matter how often he did that, my stomach never failed to do a couple of flips.

"How long can you stay?"

I studied him thoughtfully, trying to gauge whether he wanted me to stay or go. He was impossible to read as always, so I gave up.

"Let's play it by ear."

He nodded and took a sip of his coffee. I tested my tea. Still too hot.

"You ever notice there's a really short window on tea?" I asked him.

"Excuse me?"

"It's true. If it's too hot, you can't enjoy the taste, and when it gets cold, it's just unpalatable. Unless it's iced tea, then it's delicious. But you know what I mean."

Matt burst out laughing.

"What do you want to do today? Maja's gone, Greg's not back until tomorrow night. The weekend is all ours."

"How about the Heineken factory?" I suggested. "I'm in the mood for something light, touristy, and where I'll be drunk by noon."

Matt pulled out his phone and checked the site. He booked two tickets and put his phone down.

"We've got an hour. Plenty of time for you to drink your tea."

I picked up the cup, gingerly took a sip, and grimaced.

"Too cold."

CHAPTER TWELVE

The weeks flew by.

Matt worked hard during the week and I barely saw him in daylight hours. Our lunches vanished so I spent my days exploring the city and writing in various cafes and coffee shops— the latter always proving more productive.

I loved my work and threw myself into it wholeheartedly. Matt and I were certainly having enough sex that I had plenty of material to choose from or sometimes weave together if I felt like spoiling my readers. My popularity grew and I wondered if this would be it for me, if I'd end up as an erotica writer. I hadn't even told my parents yet.

The revolving door of roommates was a

never-ending source of entertainment for both of us. We got to meet so many people from all over the world—it was absolutely fascinating.

I was sitting on the couch one afternoon with Andre, a particularly fine specimen of a man from Haiti who was traveling across the continent in search of inspiration for his poetry. From my limited perspective of the previous three days, I'd say he was finding it between the legs of tall, thin, blond girls.

We were sharing a joint and he was reading me some of his latest work. It was breathtaking. A form of beat poetry with a throwback to Wordsworth-era English mixed with the patois of his birth country. I was completely swept up in the moment—his words mixed with the weed was making me positively swoon.

He was reading a particularly passionate piece when Matt walked through the front door. I was lying in the corner seat of the couch, my feet up on Andre's lap as he read. Matt just stood there for a moment and studied us, and I watched as his expression changed from tense to bewildered to something undecipherable and then finally settle on happiness at seeing me.

He walked over, leaned down, and in one move, kissed me on the mouth and took the joint from my hand. He stood back up and took a toke as he kicked off his shoes.

"How's it going, Andre?" Matt asked.

"Pretty good, man. Three more days here, making the most of it," Andre said.

"I can see that." Matt said.

He dropped down onto the couch beside me and I immediately pulled my legs down from Andre's lap and cuddled up against Matt. He kissed the top of my head and I let out a little sigh.

"Andre was just reading me some of his poetry. It's really amazing," I said.

Matt just nodded and took another toke. It was strange—he wasn't the jealous type. I couldn't understand where this mood was coming from. I ran my finger along his thigh, hoping to distract him and maybe cheer him up a little. Andre closed his journal and stood up.

"Well, that's my cue. I'm heading out for the evening. I'll see you two in the morning." And with that, Andre walked out the door.

I reached over and took the joint from Matt's hand. We sat silently for a few minutes and just smoked, passing the joint back and forth between us. As the minutes passed, I felt the tension leave his body.

"Everything okay?" I asked.

"Yeah. Everything's fine."

"Work was okay?"

"Work was fine."

We sat in silence for a few more minutes. I didn't want to push him. I closed my eyes and rested against him, wrapping my arms around his waist and leaning my head on his chest.

"What were you and Andre doing?" Matt asked out of the blue.

"I told you. He was reading his poetry."

"Why were you lying on him?"

"I was not lying on him. I was lying on the couch and when he came to sit down he moved my feet. Nothing sinister was going on. I promise you."

"He makes me nervous."

"Because he's hot. And sexy as fuck. I don't blame you. I'd be nervous about him around my girl, too. But you don't have to worry because I'm not interested in him. I'm interested in you."

I untangled myself from his body and got onto my knees, facing him. He put both hands on my waist and looked into my eyes. I leaned over and kissed his scar.

"I didn't think you were the jealous type," I said.

"I'm not."

"So, what's this all about?"

"Nothing."

My ass, it's nothing. But I knew better than to push him. He'd been a little off ever since finding out about Temple Fraser, and I figured I just had to give him some time to adjust. A delightful thought entered my head and I gazed at him with an exquisitely wicked gleam in my eye.

"Would you feel better if you spanked me?"

He dropped his hands, sat up straight, and took in a sharp breath. I reached over and ran my hand up his thigh, between his legs, instantly getting my answer.

"That's what I thought."

I stood and walked towards the bedroom, removing items of clothing as I went. First the top came off, and I looked over my shoulder at him as I tossed it aside. I took a few more steps before sliding my hands under the waist of my pants and easing them down over my legs, stepping gingerly out of them as I continued on my way.

This left me in a pair of white lace bikini underwear and a matching push-up bra. I ran my hand down my side and then over my ass, turning back towards the bedroom and walking inside. Matt stood up, as if in a daze, and followed me. As he walked through the door, I was searching through the night table drawer for the leather paddle.

I walked over to him, handed him the paddle, and climbed up onto the bed, positioning myself on all fours, pushing my ass towards him. I was already so wet and so turned on I thought I might come the moment the paddle made contact.

Matt just stood there, breathing heavily, watching me sway as I anticipated the strike. He put the paddle down and slowly undressed. He stood there, utterly naked and completely erect. He picked up the paddle and surveyed my behind. He swallowed.

"Go ahead, Matt. I want it. I want you to spank me."

He hesitated.

"Feel how wet I am. Just touch me."

He reached underneath me, stroking his fingers lightly between my legs, not even bothering to push aside my panties. I moaned, writhing against his hand. He made a guttural noise deep in his chest and pulled his hand back.

"Allie..."

"It's okay, Matt. It's not my first rodeo. I'll tell you if it's too much."

With that, I felt the first crack of the paddle. I cried out, not in pain, really, but more in surprise. Matt groaned and raised the paddle again. I arched my back, begging him with my body for another strike. He didn't disappoint, and I gasped. The initial sting was fading, quickly replaced by rising arousal.

Matt paused to peel down my underwear, leaving it just above my knees, binding my legs together. He ran his hand over my ass, stroking it, squeezing it, and finally, bringing down the paddle for another spanking.

"Oh, god. Matt. Oh my god…"

I thought I was going to pass out, and I searched frantically for an anchor. My eyes landed on his cock—hard, waiting, beautiful. I reached out and took him in my hand as I heard his sharp intake of breath. I repositioned myself so I could get him in my mouth and set to work. I was running my tongue up the underside of him when I felt the paddle land, catching me completely by surprise. I took him back in my mouth, sucking hard, pulling him in deeper.

I heard the paddle drop as he grabbed both my shoulders, grinding his hips as I moved my mouth over him. I reached up to cup his balls when suddenly, he pulled himself away. In one move, he flipped me around and so I was facing away from him and slid into me from behind. I cried out as he began to thrust.

With one hand on my ass, his other hand reached around to find my clitoris. Rather than rubbing it, he took it between his thumb and forefinger, alternately squeezing and letting go. The effect, coupled with his continued pounding, sent me over the edge and I grabbed the bedsheets as the orgasm rocked through my body. To my surprise, he pulled out and came on my ass. It was incredibly hot, but also totally unexpected.

We collapsed onto the bed and lay silently, staring up at the ceiling. After a moment I heard the pillow rustle as he turned to look at me. I faced him and smiled. He gave me a funny smirk.

"Write about that," he said.

CHAPTER THIRTEEN

So I wasn't crazy. I knew something had been different. The fucker was performing for me. He couldn't get the idea of the column out of his head. I wondered briefly if he thought I was lining Andre up to be material.

I quickly discarded that thought, realizing such thinking would only lead me down a dangerous path. He was just insecure, that was all. It would take him some time. I glanced over at him, but he was sound asleep, without a care in the world. I looked around, helpless, wishing more than anything Lynn would suddenly appear at my bedside.

I turned to look at my phone and realized it was a decent hour back home. I jumped out of bed and walked into the living room, dialing her as I went. She picked up right away.

"What's wrong?" Lynn asked.

"You know me so well."

"Surprise FaceTime is not your style. What happened?"

"Matt found out about my side gig."

"Oy. And?"

"Well, he says he's okay with it, but he seems to be...doing things a little differently in the bedroom. Like he's trying to impress me."

"Typical male ego."

"He's not like that."

"All men are like that. All people are like that. You cannot convince me otherwise. How is he outside the bedroom?"

"Weird."

"What's the relationship status at this point?"

"Confused?"

"Christ, Allie. Do you need me to fly out there?"

I perked up.

"Would you?" I asked.

"No, I would not. Although it does sound like fun. Listen to me. You've got to read the room and figure out how to handle this. I'm not there and I've only got your side of the story. Give him some leeway, don't let him be a dick. It's not that difficult."

"I guess not. Maybe I just needed to hear it."

Lynn laughed and shook her head, sending her long waves out fanning. Only she could look glamorous on a video call.

"How's Amsterdam?" she asked.

"It's fantastic. I don't know if I'd live here, but it would certainly be an easy adjustment. All the food, the culture, the weed…it's the perfect city for me."

"Have you seen a sex show?"

"Oh, yes. And we went to a peep show."

"GET OUT!"

"Dirtiest sex I ever had."

"IN THE BOOTH?"

I could practically see down Lynn's throat she was screaming so loud.

"Where are you?" I asked.

"At the grocery store."

I burst out laughing. She tilted the phone away, towards the long lines of cans—beans and other legumes, from what I could tell. As she turned it back towards herself, I caught the faces of a few amused shoppers. I rolled my eyes.

"You could have told me or gone somewhere a little more private."

"Oh, come on. It's not every day strangers get to hear stories of sex in peep-show booths."

I felt myself blush, even though I was alone on the couch in our living room, thousands of miles and an ocean away from any of those people. I distracted myself by grabbing the box from the coffee table and rolling a joint.

"How are things back home?" I asked.

There was a pause.

"Things are…good."

"Spill it."

"Well, I think I might have met someone."

"WHAT? How did you not lead with that?"

"You called me, remember?"

"Right. Okay, who is it?"

There was silence. I stopped rolling for a moment and looked at Lynn through the phone propped up on the table.

"Hello? Spill it, woman."

"Well, it's nothing I intended to happen. And I'm going to pull a you and opt not to talk about it right now. I'm allowed to do that, right?"

Lynn stopped for a moment to let that sink in and I leaned back on the couch and lit my joint.

"I guess you are."

I sat smoking while Lynn went through the checkout. A few minutes passed and she pulled the phone out of her pocket again. She was sitting outside on a bench in the snow under the moonlight.

"Cold?" I asked.

"Not so much. It's been a pretty mild winter. When are you coming home?"

The sudden change in subject made me pause.

"I don't know," I said. "I guess that all depends on how the next couple of weeks play out. If he can get used to this whole thing or not. But you're right. I'll give him leeway, and make sure he's not an asshole."

"Thatta girl."

I laughed.

"I better go if I want to get any sleep tonight. Love you."

"Love you, too."

I put out the joint, walked back into the bedroom, and crawled into bed. I snuggled under the duvet and looked over at Matt, who was fast asleep. I knew he liked me. We had fun together. I just had to give it some time. It was all my fault, anyway—I should have told him right from the beginning. But who knew it would become such a big thing?

I reached out and gently pushed the hair off his forehead. He was incredibly good looking. I smiled to myself, rolled over, and went to sleep.

CHAPTER FOURTEEN

We fell into a groove over the next few weeks, spending days apart and nights together. I was still a little on edge. Matt hadn't really given me anything I could point to and say, "Look, there, you did that," so there was no opening for the conversation. I knew flat out accusing him of anything would be a big mistake. I may have not known much about men, but that I knew.

Yet I still felt things were off. I was hyper-aware every time we had sex, trying to figure out if he was in the moment or playing by some script. It was driving me crazy. I was constantly second-guessing myself and him. And he knew something was up with me but was likewise walking on eggshells. It made for some interesting evenings.

"Let's go for a walk," Matt suggested one evening in late December. It was close to Christmas and we were just hanging out on the couch after a dinner of Indian takeout. While the Dutch didn't exactly celebrate the way we did in North America, they seemed to have made an effort in order to satisfy their tourists. There was a Christmas Square in the Museumplein we'd heard about that we wanted to see.

"We'll walk around, rent some ice skates, have a good old-fashioned winter date."

I smiled up at him.

"I love it," I said.

We grabbed our jackets and hit the street. Matt took my hand and kissed the top of my head when we stopped for a light at the corner. I smiled, allowing myself to enjoy the moment. Being with him was just fun. And it had been so easy—certainly it would be that way again.

As we walked from the flat to the Museumplein, Matt told me about the past few weeks at work. He'd started opening up about his job recently, something I took as a good sign. We spoke so little about what was going on between us that I was constantly searching for clues in his actions. Letting me into his professional world was a good clue.

Matt was only two months away from the end of his contract. My writing was going great and I'd decided, with Trish's enthusiastic approval, to stay with him for the duration. I missed Loki and Lynn dreadfully. I'd even reached the point where I was missing my parents. But how often would I have a chance like this?

My attention drifted back to Matt, in time to catch him mentioning Israel.

"What? I'm sorry. I drifted there for a moment."

"I was just saying it looks like Jeff is really screwing up the job in Israel. It's a good thing I'll be done here sooner rather than later. Things are going so smoothly I may be able to finish early."

"But how can you help him any more from home than you can from here?"

Matt just looked at me.

"I'd have to go there."

"To Israel?"

Matt nodded.

"For how long?"

Matt shrugged.

"Not sure. I need to spend some time at home first, assess the damage and see where he went wrong. Or where the client screwed up.

Then I'd have a better idea."

I nodded slowly. He did tell me he traveled often.

"I did tell you I traveled often."

I couldn't help but laugh out loud. He took that as encouragement. We walked in silence for a bit.

"Allie," he started.

"Yeah?"

"Would you tell me about the, well, about the spanking? The whole paddle and crop business? I mean, I don't want to pry, but I've got to admit. I'm curious. Josh?"

I laughed.

"No," I said, catching my breath. "Definitely not Josh. Much too straight for that. Josh was great in bed—but straight up vanilla. No, that was just something I experimented with a little after college. Couple of guys I dated over the span of a year."

Matt nods, thinking.

"And you enjoy it?" he asked.

"At times," I answered, my defenses up. "You don't seem to mind it much yourself."

He stopped and looked at me, taking my arm so I'm forced to stop as well.

"Hey, I wasn't judging. I was just making sure. Yes, I enjoy it. Yes, like you, not all the time. I'm just checking to see if we're on the same page here."

I relaxed a little, visibly apparently because he was content to let it go. When we hit the market, we both stopped short in utter awe. It was beautiful. The entire area, usually bare when not in service to an event, was entirely lit up—strings of lights wrapped around bare tree boughs, stalls and carousels brightly decorated and glowing with colour. In the centre of it all was the skating rink, filled with families and lovers, skating hand in hand.

Matt wrapped his arms around my waist from behind and rested his chin on the top of my head.

"Well."

"Well," I agreed.

It was night, and save for the festive lighting, the square was dark. There were bodies everywhere, and we slid stealthily between them, seeing the sights and checking out the vendors' wares. We bought nothing. Our hands were tightly entwined, the heat building up between us as we moved through the market.

We found ourselves at the corner of Museumplein and Museumpromenade, at the very edge of the market.

"Where are you going?" I asked him, though honestly I was content to be led wherever he desired.

"Just come. I see a spot up ahead."

He led me up to the edge of a gathering of trees that lined that edge of the square. The end of the square and the busy boulevard on one side, all the action of the market on the other. We slid into the trees, unnoticed and completely giddy.

I was laughing softly when his hands reached up and cupped my face. I looked up at him as he leaned in to kiss me, covering my mouth with his own. I fell into the kiss, taking a step towards him without breaking contact. My hands found their way around to his back, settling on his ass as I pulled him closer. He increased the intensity of his kiss as I arched my back, pressing my chest into his. The butterflies in my stomach exploded in all directions, my head so light I thought I'd faint.

"What is it about Christmas that makes me so horny?" he whispered in my ear, breathless.

"It's the thought of spending it with a shicksa," I said, laughing.

In truth, I didn't know if he'd ever dated a non-Jewish girl before, but it didn't really matter. He groaned somewhere deep in his throat and kissed me again, this time pushing me up against a tree. He broke away, pushing the hair from my face and letting his hand fall to my breast, casually tracing my nipple with his finger.

"Are you a dirty shicksa?" he asked.

"That depends. What did you have in mind?"

Matt reached over and pulled down the zipper on my jeans. I looked at him in shock.

"Are you nuts? We're outside. There are people around."

"No one can see us."

He undid the button and gave me a wicked grin.

"It's winter."

"You're from the North East and it's four degrees above zero. It's practically balmy."

He leaned over and bit my breast through my jacket. I moaned. He looked up at me and smiled. I tried to push him away, but he leaned in and whispered in my ear.

"Besides, I have a feeling if I reached into your pants right now, I'd find you very, very ready."

I moaned again, pressing my body against him. He took my earlobe between his teeth, nibbling gently as I eased down his jeans.

"That's my girl," he whispered.

He pulled away and, hooking his fingers into my waistband, took down my pants in a flash. I stood there in my jacket and lace bikinis, jeans around my ankles, as he stared at me, the hunger clear in his eyes. He dropped to his knees, ducked his head under my legs and took hold of my hips, burying himself in me. I rested my head against the tree behind me, feeling him push aside my panties as his tongue found its way home.

I rested on his shoulders, placing the bulk of my weight against the tree with my back. He reached up, placing his hands under my ass to better support me, and redoubled his efforts. I wrapped my fingers in his hair, panting as he lightly bit, then sucked, my clitoris. I made circles with my hips, each time bringing myself closer and closer to him until he grabbed my ass and buried his fingers deep, causing me to cry out.

My eyes flew open as the orgasm took over my body. He refused to let up, causing the waves to wash over me again and again as I cried his name, barely audible over the music on the other side of the trees. I heard him moan and knew he was far from done. As he ducked back out from under my legs and straightened up, I saw a couple at the edge of the woods, staring at us.

As Matt lowered his underwear and moved in towards me, I whispered in his ear.

"Matt, there are people there."

"So what," he murmured, nuzzling my neck as he wrapped his arms around my bare waist. I felt him grind against me, the smell of sex surrounding us. He leaned in and kissed me, and I could taste myself on him, causing me to momentarily forget the couple in the woods.

"They're watching us," I said as I regained my senses.

Matt looked back over his shoulder and saw them. They stood there, a man and woman, probably in their mid-thirties, just watching us as they held hands. As we looked at them, the man raised his hand, brushing it over the woman's breast, tracing her nipple, similar to what Matt had done to me earlier. How long had they been watching?

Matt turned back to me and watched my face as I stared at them. No one was moving.

"Does it turn you on? Having them watch?"

"I don't know. I think it might."

"Let them watch."

Matt reached down and guided himself into me. I got up on my tiptoes and tilted my hips upwards to meet him. He reached under and cupped my ass, pushing me up against the tree as he bit my neck.

"I want to hear you scream," he whispered in my ear.

With that, he pulled back and thrust himself

into me with such force that I did scream. I called out to him, to God, and possibly for mercy, as he fucked me against that tree, under the stars of a mild winter's night in Amsterdam. Now *this* was a side of Matt I could get used to.

When he was done, he pulled out and leaned in to nuzzle my neck, pausing on his way up to kiss the top of my head. I wrapped my arms around him, savouring the smell of him and letting it fill my senses.

"You're amazing," he whispered.

"You're amazing."

"They still watching?"

I was confused, having momentarily forgotten about the couple. I raised my eyes and looked over Matt's shoulder, but there was no one there.

"Gone," I said.

"I hope they saw you finish. That was quite a finish."

I may have blushed. Matt bent down to pull up his pants and grabbed mine while he was at it. I rested against the tree, looking down at him as he carefully zipped and buttoned me up. He was adorable.

"Come," he said, standing up. "Let's go skating."

CHAPTER FIFTEEN

Our living situation, while admittedly strange, was also a lot of fun. It kind of felt like we were on a never-ending first date. I mean, we were living together, for all intents and purposes, but we weren't at either of our apartments, and we were in a strange city, so it felt more like *vacationing* together than anything else. Except it had been almost four months. And we were both working.

For the most part, we got along famously. Matt was much neater than I was, but I was content to let him pick up after me. The constant turnover of roommates kept things fresh and sometimes gave us a chance to play tour guide/tourist for a few days now and then.

And then there were the precious days when there were no roommates and we had the entire place to ourselves.

On one such morning, I was in the bathroom, dressed in my T-shirt and underwear, brushing my teeth. Matt knocked on the door.

"Yes?" I said.

He opened the door and walked in, dressed only in his boxers. He picked up his toothbrush.

"What are you doing?" I asked.

"Brushing my teeth."

"Yes doesn't mean 'come in,' you know."

"It doesn't?"

"No."

"Oh."

He kissed the top of my head before squeezing the toothpaste onto his brush. I rinsed, spat, and turned to him.

"What if I'd been peeing?" I asked.

"So what?"

I rolled my eyes at him.

"Listen, I know it feels like we've been living together forever, but in fact, we've only been dating for four months. We've gotten very intimate, very fast."

He listened as he brushed.

"I'm not saying that's bad," I continued.

"I'm just saying maybe some things are best kept a mystery for now."

He spat and looked at me.

"You don't like me in the bathroom?" he asked, amused.

I smiled.

"I do like you in the bathroom."

He ran his hands up my belly, pushing my shirt out of the way as he went. He took hold and pulled it up over my head, leaving me in just my panties. He gazed at me with soft eyes, turning my insides to jelly.

"God, you're so beautiful."

"You make me feel beautiful."

The corner of his mouth pulled up in a smile and I reached out to trace the scar over his eye. I closed my eyes as my fingers memorized the lines and the feel of it. I felt his fingers close around my wrist as he gently pulled my hand aside and leaned in to kiss me.

Some things in this world got boring over time. Have pasta for dinner every night, you'll get sick of pasta. But Matt's kisses were something else altogether. Each one was better than the last. He had a goddess-given talent that made me weak in the knees every time.

I parted my lips and felt his tongue greet my own. I smiled against his mouth, and he pulled me in close. I still had my back up against the vanity, ass resting against the sink. I felt his hands reach around me and then he was pulling away. I looked down to see him pouring some hand cream into his palm.

He looked me in the eye and rubbed his hands together. I lifted my own hands and rested them on his shoulders, enjoying the feeling of his muscles rippling beneath my fingertips. Once again I closed my eyes, running my hands across the top of his back. I felt his hands on my chest, carefully rubbing the cream into my breasts, causing me to writhe against the sink.

"Allie," he moaned as he worked the cream into my skin. He took my nipples between his fingers, rolling them, squeezing and pulling until I thought I wouldn't be able to bear it for one more second. Then he leaned forward and took one breast in his mouth. I sighed, arching my back, and was alarmed when he pulled away suddenly.

"Christ, that tastes terrible."

I burst out laughing.

"I imagine it would," I said.

He made a face, wrinkling his nose and reaching around me to spit into the sink.

"Here," I said. "Let me fix it."

I got up on my tippy toes and kissed him again, running my hands through his hair and rubbing my now very slippery breasts against his bare chest. He ran his hands up my sides, stopping at my breasts for a squeeze and then continuing onto my back. He pulled away and put his hands on my hips, turning me around to face the sink and the mirror.

I braced my hands on the vanity as he slid my panties down over my thighs. He ran his hands over my ass as he stood back up. He leaned in over my shoulder, lips grazing my ear.

"Look at me," he said with both tenderness and force.

I opened my eyes and stared straight into his reflection in the mirror. I felt his hands tighten on my hips, and then I felt him slide in. I was so wet he needed absolutely zero guidance. His eyelids fluttered momentarily, and I grinned, savouring the knowledge that I'd made him feel that way.

He fucked me slowly, but it was still fucking. The way he held my eyes as he thrust into me, the way he squeezed my hips. I let my eyes drop a fraction and stared at my breasts in the mirror, watching them heave with each breath, seeing my nipples hard as rocks, staring back at me. I brought my gaze back up to his eyes, only to discover he'd also been watching my breasts.

"Please," I whispered. "Touch them."

His hands left my hips and I grabbed the countertop even tighter, taking over the bulk of the work for him, rolling my hips up and pushing my ass towards him, ready to take him over and over again. His hands found my breasts, and as we both watched, he held them and squeezed them, running his thumb over my nipples, making me even wetter.

Being with him, whether it was on a romantic houseboat or up against the bathroom sink, was always an erotic adventure. He had come to understand my body so intimately in such a short time. His touch on my skin was enough to waken every nerve. And he knew it.

"Matt... oh, god, Matt..."

He dropped one hand between my legs and moaned when he felt how wet I was. He continued fucking me as his hand found my clitoris, using his thumb to press hard while his finger rubbed me from underneath. It was just enough to send me over the edge.

"Look at me."

I brought my eyes back up to the mirror, desperately trying to keep my eyes open as I came violently around both his cock and his hand.

"Oh, god, Matt..."

I felt his final thrust, and he collapsed against

my back, holding me tight as his own orgasm wracked through his body.

CHAPTER SIXTEEN

I was sitting at the kitchen table working on my latest piece when I got distracted by my phone ringing. I figured it was Matt, calling to see what I wanted for dinner. I reached for the phone and was about to answer when I saw the caller ID. Josh.

I swallowed hard, dropping the phone on the table as if it were in flames. I just stared at it, completely paralyzed. Why was he calling me? After what seemed like an eternity, the phone stopped ringing. I stared at it, waiting for the voicemail light to come on. It never did. Instead, I heard the familiar buzz of a text message and saw his name on the bubble flash on my screen.

I closed my eyes, swallowed again, took a deep breath, and opened my eyes. I picked up the phone and unlocked it, bracing myself to read the message. *Allie. Call me. I want to talk.*

I immediately deleted the text. What on earth was he thinking? I reached for the extinguished joint in the ashtray on the table and re-lit it. Josh. I watched the smoke curl up around my head. Josh. I shook my head and took another drag. No. I would not go there. I had no idea what he wanted, but I did not intend to find out.

I put the joint back in the ashtray and got back to my work. I had managed to put the whole thing out of my mind and was working on a particularly steamy scene when I heard the front door open and shut.

"In here," I called.

I heard Matt drop his keys on the entryway table and make his way to the kitchen. He had such a distinctive gait. I rolled my eyes. Now I found his gait charming? Lynn would just laugh at me at this point. Truth be told, I was very happy to see him when he walked through the kitchen door. He looked very tasty. Bonus points that he was carrying a bottle of champagne.

"Hey, you," he said, leaning down to kiss me on the head.

"Hey, yourself. How was your day?"

He didn't answer me for a moment as he stood reading over my shoulder. I blushed slightly. I knew he was now reading my stories, but it was one thing for him to read them on the website, and a whole other thing for him to be reading one in front of me.

"Museumplein?" he asked.

"Yup."

"That was a good one."

He put down the bottle and mystery takeout bag. From the smell I would guess pasta of some sort, but I couldn't be sure. He started pulling out containers. Yup. Pasta.

"What's the champers for?" I asked.

He looked down at me and smiled.

"Ah. I've got some good news."

I closed my laptop and gave him my full attention. Well, as much as I could. By now it was quite evident to both of us what was on my mind. He laughed.

"I'll take care of you in a moment," he said, shaking his head in amusement. "Funny job hazard you've got there. But first, I'd like to toast and eat first, if that's okay."

I shrugged and got up to get some glasses. We were well stocked, but champagne flutes were a big ask. I settled for the wine glasses. I held them out as he popped the cork and poured.

"So?" I asked. "What are we toasting?"

"I'm done."

"Done?"

"Done. Four weeks ahead of schedule. We can be home as early as next week."

I put my glass down, stunned. The realization that I'd been living in a fantasy world came crashing down around me as I contemplated somehow transporting this relationship back home and keeping it intact.

"We're leaving Amsterdam?"

Matt put down his glass as well, troubled by my reaction.

"Well, you knew we were going to at some point."

"Yes, but that point was four, five weeks away. Now you're telling me it's next week."

"I thought you'd be happy. Loki. Your apartment. Your family. Lynn! And you've lost weight—it's time to get back to restaurant reviews, no?"

I looked at him.

"I, for one, miss all those free meals," he said, trying to make light of the situation.

I sat back down. He studied me, tilting his head to the side. Then he knelt on the floor by my chair, taking my hands in his.

"What's bothering you?"

"What happens to us when we get home?"

There. I'd said it. Us. The one topic we'd managed to avoid all this time. What would happen to us?

"What do you even mean? Nothing will happen to us, Allie. I'm here, with you. I'll be there, with you. Wherever I am, I'm with you. I thought that was clear at this point."

"And when you're in Israel?"

"When I'm in Israel? Is that what this is about?"

I could've kicked myself. He just basically confirmed we were committed and already I started nagging.

"No. That's not what this is about. You're right. I'm being silly. This is great news. For everyone. Except Trish, I suppose."

I took his face in my hands and kissed him.

"What's for dinner?" I asked.

He stood up, still watching me, unsure.

"I'm fine, Matt. You just caught me by surprise. You're right. We'll be great back home. I know we will."

"Pasta," he said.

*

I was wrapping up a few fragile items I'd bought in bubble wrap before packing them in a box to send home. Matt was going through his clothes, trying to figure out what to bring home and what to donate before leaving.

"Should I throw the sex toys in the box?" I asked.

"Uh, yeah. You want to explain them in your luggage?"

"Good point."

I wrapped them in newspaper and threw them in with the other stuff.

"Did you remove the batteries?" he asked.

I laughed and fished them out again, taking care to remove the batteries. He knew me well.

"What do you want to do today? Your choice," Matt said.

"Totally my choice?"

"One hundred percent."

"I want to take you to see the *Night Watch*."

Matt groaned.

"Matt. You've been here for five months. In the same city as one of the most famous and magnificent paintings in the world. And you haven't seen it. You haven't even set foot in the museum that houses it. I've lost count of the times I've been there. Please. Come see it."

"Fine. If it will make you happy. But then can we go get drunk and fuck somewhere along the canal?"

"If you insist," I said.

Deception

"Give me five minutes to shower."

CHAPTER SEVENTEEN

It was a relatively cold afternoon for Amsterdam. We were dressed in jeans and light jackets for the walk to the Rijksmuseum and we were both feeling the chill. Matt took my hand and nodded towards an upcoming coffee shop.

"Why don't we duck inside?" he suggested.

"Matt..."

"Come on, it's freezing out here. We'll warm up. You say you've been to this museum countless times, but how many times have you been there high?"

"Never," I admitted.

"So? Just imagine. If you love it so much, it'll be even better when you're stoned."

I realized I was asking him to do something he was not crazy about. Matt loved to read, was happy to watch movies and, from our conversations, I knew he'd seen at least a handful of award-winning plays. He was up on his politics and his social issues, and he was definitely intelligent. So I knew there was culture there, but clearly old paintings weren't his cup of tea. So, I conceded and followed him into the coffee shop.

We stood there for a moment, getting warm and getting our bearings. It was a pretty nondescript place, but the overwhelming smell of good pot was enough for us to grab a seat and look at the menu. Matt selected a bud when the waiter came by and we sat back, just looking at each other.

"What?" I asked.

"I'm just enjoying you," he said.

"People don't say things like that, you know."

"I do."

"I know you do."

I leaned across the table and kissed him. When the waiter returned, Matt got to work rolling and we sat and smoked in silence for a while, people-watching.

"So," he said. "Have you come to terms with it yet?"

I stiffened slightly but was determined not to let anything ruin the day.

"Yes. Of course. I've already spoken to Sarah and she's happy to have me back. You'll get the curves back in no time."

"Mmm. Where will we go first? Or were you serious when you told Pete you don't take your dates out for dinner?"

"Of course I'll take you for dinner, you idiot. Speaking of dinner, where will we eat after?"

"I was thinking we'd walk over to the Waterhole in the Leidsplein. They've got a great happy hour that goes from noon until nine. We'll get there in plenty of time to catch a few hours of cheap booze. It's only a ten-minute walk."

"Do they have food there?"

"Well, they have bar snacks."

I looked at him.

"Fine, we'll grab some drinks then hit a real restaurant for dinner."

I smiled.

"Sounds great."

We stood up, grabbed our coats, and headed to the museum.

When we got there, we were both in a very giggly mood. Whatever weed Matt had ordered had definitely been an upper. The guy at the admission booth was a little unsure about us, and I couldn't say I blamed him. As I reached across for our tickets, Matt squeezed my ass with such ferocity I squealed.

I took him on a very abbreviated tour of my favourite paintings, ending up, of course, at the *Night Watch*. He stood there for a while, staring at it. Then he looked at me and shrugged. Even after a lengthy description and a brief history of Rembrandt, he was completely unimpressed. I was forced to admit that for all his great qualities, Matt did not appreciate the Dutch masters.

We left the museum and walked to the Waterhole. Just as I was in awe that he'd never been to the Rijksmuseum, he couldn't believe I'd spent four months in the city without wandering into that tourist trap.

We walked in and found two seats at the bar. Matt ordered a couple of shots, indicating he was serious about getting trashed. I was still flying from the weed but figured what the hell, we were certainly in for a good night. We downed the shots and he looked at the drink menu.

"They've only got Beefeater."

"Forget it," I said. "Surprise me with something else."

"May I offer you a drink?"

Matt and I looked at each other before I

turned to see who was talking to me. I swiveled in my stool and saw a very familiar-looking man on the seat next to me.

"Do I know you?" I asked.

He laughed softly.

"I should think so. Although you were a little distracted when we, uh, met. I don't believe we had the opportunity to exchange names at the time. I'm James."

I looked back at Matt, who shrugged, clearly just as confused as I was. I turned back and put out my hand.

"Allie."

"Allie. Lovely name. You look…very different with clothes on."

And that's when it hit me. This was the man who had been watching us in the woods at the Christmas market. Holy shit. I turned back to Matt and saw the realization had struck him, too. He reached out and put his hand around my waist, pulling me closer in a subtle but clear fashion. James noticed.

"Don't worry, mate. I'm not here to take your woman. I just thought you two might be up for some fun."

I felt a stirring very deep in my loins. I don't know if it was the weed, the booze, the combination of the two, but it was not something I wanted to explore. I quashed the feeling down and took a step even closer to Matt.

Just at that moment, James' girlfriend walked up. She took one look at us, and then at James, and raised her eyebrows in amusement.

"Well, well. What have we got here? Have you found us dates for the evening then, James?"

"Sweetheart. Meet Allie. Allie, this is Lisa, my wife."

"Your wife."

"Yes."

The two smiled at each other. Lisa broke eye contact and looked at Matt.

"And you are?"

"Matt," he said, without putting out his hand.

Lisa leaned in towards me, all conspiratorial-like.

"Allie, from what I've seen, I'd say you lucked out with this one. He certainly seems to know what he's doing."

She then reached out and ran her finger along Matt's scar. MY SCAR. I didn't move, but I felt Matt pull his face back, just a fraction. She turned to me, cupping my chin her hand.

"And you. Well, you just look like a whole lot of fun."

"Hold on there, Lisa," James said. "They

haven't agreed to anything yet. Allie hasn't even let me buy her a drink."

Lisa took a step back and James turned once more to me.

"You will let me buy you a drink, won't you?"

"Um…"

I heard Matt's voice behind me.

"What the hell," he said. "Why not?"

I looked back at him, surprised. What the hell? James signaled the waiter and ordered a round of shots, and a round of drinks. I took a deep breath. What the fuck was Matt doing? A foursome? Really? My old doubts about his performance anxiety started creeping back with a vengeance.

The drinks arrived and I picked up my shot and downed it fast. James looked over at me appreciatively and got up from his stool.

"Take my seat, sweetheart. I want to get to know Allie better," James said.

He turned to me and put out his hand.

"Come, let's get a little closer to the band."

I looked over my shoulder at Matt, but he just shrugged and picked up his drink. I widened my eyes at him, but if he noticed, he sure as hell pretended not to. So this was it? He was going to just play it cool while some other guy tried to get into my pants?

I thought about putting my foot down right then and there. But then I got mad. Fuck him. After everything we'd been through, if he was still so insecure about a fucking website, there was nothing I could do to help him.

I followed James towards the stage and we took up a spot to listen. He put his hand on my back and while the music played he made slow circles, edging closer and closer towards my ass. I grew more and more aggravated. Not with James. I couldn't give a fuck about James. But with Matt. Where the hell was he? Why wasn't he here, pulling me away? Telling me he was sorry? Did he want to have a foursome?

I looked back towards the bar to see if I could see him and Lisa. For all I knew, he might have been making out with her already. I was suddenly confused, unsure of whether we were in this situation because Matt was upset about my writing, or because he saw an opportunity for an experience he'd always wanted and just figured I'd be game.

I tried to look at James in a new light. He was attractive. Tall, dark, with beautiful black eyes. I'd never seen eyes so dark before. He caught me staring and smiled, showing off a set of perfect teeth. Could I fuck him?

James looked over at me, amused.

"Would you like to go back to the bar? See

what our partners are up to?"

I nodded, completely unable to speak.

I followed him back to the bar, trying to prepare myself for whatever we might find. Matt and Lisa were just drinking and talking. Matt looked up as we approached, studying me carefully.

"Maybe it's time to get out of here," James said.

Lisa jumped up and put on her jacket. I looked at Matt, who just shrugged.

"Sure," he said. "Why not?"

He handed me my jacket as he put on his own. I pulled mine on slowly, watching his every move.

"This is what you want?" I whispered to him.

"Absolutely," he said, kissing the top of my head.

Huh.

We walked out of the bar and hit the streets. James told us their rental was only a block or two away, so we walked north with them. I stumbled on the pavement, and Lisa was by my side, quick as a flash. She slid an arm around my waist to support me, and we walked together.

We stopped at the corner to wait for traffic and I looked over at her. It was all the encouragement she needed, and she leaned in and kissed me.

"Now, now, Lisa." James scolded. "Be patient."

He took my hand and gently led me away. The light changed and we continued across the street. I looked over at Matt, who was speaking in low voices with Lisa. We arrived at their apartment and followed them up the steps and through the door.

It was a charming place, much smaller than Matt's. It was entirely open concept, and a king-sized bed was in plain sight at the far end of the room. James stood in front of me and unzipped my jacket. He peeled it slowly off my shoulders and then leaned over to kiss me. His tongue felt foreign and odd, but I barely had time to contemplate it before he pulled away to take off his own jacket.

I turned to Matt, who was just standing there, staring at me. I looked at him, helpless. If this was what he wanted, I wanted to do this for him. But he was just standing there, totally unreadable. I looked down at his pants, to see if I could get some answer there. There appeared to be zero action.

"Matt. Come."

He stood there, shaking his head.

"This is what you want? Just to watch me?"

He nodded.

James took my chin in his hand and turned me towards him for another kiss. Lisa moved in, and James turned to kiss her. I looked towards Matt again. He was looking less sure.

"Really?" I asked.

His face broke, a mix of frustration and regret moving in. He took a step towards me, then stopped.

"No," he said. "But I bet this will make for some great stories."

That stopped me cold. James and Lisa instantly sensed something had changed. They took a step backwards as I crossed the room towards Matt.

"So this is about the column."

He didn't say a word.

"Matt. What the fuck? I thought you wanted this. For you. I didn't want this for me. I… I…"

I looked back at James and Lisa, suddenly very sober, and very angry. I grabbed my jacket and stormed out the front door. Despite the cold, I walked all the way back to our flat, grateful that we were currently alone, the next tenant not due to arrive until after our departure. I climbed the steps, turned the key in the lock, and headed straight for the bedroom. I stopped short just outside the door.

I turned around and walked through the living room. I'd sleep in the spare room tonight.

*

I woke the next morning, feeling exactly as I should have—like crap. I was getting too old to smoke and drink like I was still twenty. As the pounding subsided, the memories of what had transpired the night before came back. I covered my face with my hands and resigned myself to the fact I'd have to talk to Matt.

I slid out of bed and, after making a quick stop in the bathroom, walked to his bedroom, giving a quick knock before entering. It was empty. He'd clearly been there because the sheets were messy, and Matt Goldberg was incapable of going a day without his bed being made. I looked around, considering, trying to figure out where he could be. Giving up, I went to the kitchen to make breakfast.

I was packing up the last of my stuff when I heard Matt's key in the door. I put down the shirt I was folding and stood there for a moment, trying to decide what to do. This was going to be really awkward. I'd almost had sex with two strangers last night. In front of him. How were we to get past that? I took a deep breath and turned towards the door. He was standing right there.

"Hey," he said.

I gave him a wry smile.

"Listen," he said. "You almost had sex last night with two complete strangers. And I realize it's only because you thought it was something I wanted you to do. That's really awkward. I don't know how we get past that."

I bit my lower lip and nodded in agreement, trying to look solemn but once again amazed at his ability to read my mind.

"But I have an idea," he said.

Matt walked towards me and handed me a rectangular box, beautifully wrapped. I went to pull the ribbon, but he put out his hand to stop me.

"I want to make something clear first. I'm crazy about you. I have been since the first day I laid eyes on you. There is no one else I want. And I don't want to see you with anyone else. I wouldn't have let you go through with that."

He stopped for a moment to collect his thoughts. I waited very patiently. I mean, I was sitting there with a wrapped gift in my hands, for Christ's sake.

"When I found out about the column, I felt betrayed. I knew it was irrational. I just couldn't figure out why you wouldn't tell me.

And then we talked about it, and your explanation made sense. But at the same time, I felt this overwhelming burden that I had to be some incredible lover in order to provide you with material—"

"You are an incredible lover," I interrupted.

"Whatever. I'm just saying I felt..."

"Insecure."

"Yes. Insecure. And then I felt that maybe I wasn't enough. When you freaked out about going home, my thoughts immediately went to all our adventures here, and I worried that maybe you thought I'd be too boring at home. And you'd need something to spice it up. I don't know. I don't know, Allie. I just know I don't want to lose you. So I thought about it. And I decided if we do have to spice things up, we can do it a different way. Just the two of us."

"Matt. You're insane. Spice things up? This is the hottest sex I've ever had. You are a god. What the fuck is in this box?"

"Open it."

I pulled off the ribbon and tore the paper. I yanked off the lid, pushed aside the tissue paper, and found a beautiful pink strap-on dildo. I burst into laughter, and then I started to cry.

"What's wrong? This was supposed to be a

good thing."

I looked up at him, those green eyes staring down into mine.

"It is. It's a great thing. You're amazing."

"I'm not saying tonight. And I'm not saying I can do this without vast quantities of alcohol. But like you said, with you, I'm game to try anything."

CHAPTER EIGHTEEN

Back home on familiar ground, we stood in line at security after a long turbulent flight. While we were both thrilled to be off that plane, we were also both a little uneasy about what lay ahead. Nothing changed in my feelings for him as we stepped off the plane. In fact, I was already picturing dinner parties with Lynn and whoever her secret boyfriend was. But I wasn't naïve. I was also very aware that in a few short weeks, he'd likely be leaving for Israel.

"Penny for your thoughts," Matt said, interrupting my reverie.

More like a shekel, I thought, but said nothing.

"Hey, you okay?" Matt asked.

"I'm fine. Really. Just tired after that flight."

"Me, too. And I'm not looking forward to going back to that apartment."

I looked at him.

"You want to stay at my place tonight?" I asked.

"Allie, I want to stay at your place every night."

"NEXT!"

We both looked up as the security agent signaled us forward. I let Matt do the talking as I contemplated what he just said. He wanted to move in together. We'd been dating for four months. True, we'd lived together all that time, but that was circumstantial. This would be by choice.

Matt finished and the agent waved us through. We walked towards baggage claim to collect the luggage we'd flown with. The rest was being shipped by boat. I mulled the idea over and over in my mind. I stood watching the carousel turn, knowing from experience our bags would be the last to appear.

"Allie."

I turned to him.

"If you're worried about Israel, just come with me."

"What?"

"Why not? You did it with Amsterdam. You've got a job that lets you travel now. Come with me. I bet you've never been."

"I haven't. How long are you going for?"

"I don't know yet. Won't be longer than six months, though. And I'm due for some vacation soon. We could go to Greece. Or not. I'm just saying, don't let one upcoming trip make you second-guess everything. We have time. We don't have to make any long-term decisions now."

I'll never know what made me do it, but right then and there I decided to trust him. Why couldn't I go to Israel with him? Why couldn't we figure out a way to make this work?

"Let's do it," I said.

He gave a whoop and swept me up from around the waist and planted a deep kiss on my lips. I wrapped my arms around his neck, kissing him back and settling into the idea of being kissed like this every day. When our bags came, we gathered them all up and found a cab. I'd called Trish in advance and she knew we were coming. By the time we got home, she had cleared out. But man, was Loki happy to see us.

After she'd finished jumping up on both of us (strictly forbidden!) and licking our faces, she ran around the apartment in a state of utter bliss. I peeled off my clothes as I walked towards the bathroom, heading straight for the shower.

"Good idea," Matt said, following my lead.

I turned the tap on, testing the water before turning on the showerhead. I climbed in and Matt quickly joined suit. As I wet my hair, he reached for the shampoo and rubbed it between his hands, then lathered it into my hair.

"That feels amazing," I said.

"Lean back, I'll rinse it out."

I leaned my head back and he removed the showerhead to rinse out all the soap. When he was done, he redirected the stream so the hot water ran over my chest, cascading down my breasts. I must have let out a pleasurable sound because he chuckled under his breath.

"What?" I asked.

"Oh nothing. I've heard rumours of the pleasures a good showerhead can bring. Just never saw it in action before."

I gave him a wicked smile.

"It gets much better than that," I said.

He handed me the showerhead.

"Show me."

I took the showerhead from his hand and backed up until I was leaning up against the tile. I brought up one leg, resting the bottom of my foot on the wall and letting my knee fall open, giving him a clear view between my legs. I brought the showerhead up, letting the water rinse the last suds from my hair, and watching as they trailed down my breasts.

I then brought the showerhead down lower, aiming it directly between my legs. With the other hand, I adjusted the ring, changing the setting from cascade to jet. Matt let out a little laugh.

"So that's how you do it."

He soaped up his hand as I aimed the spray at my sweet spot, watching him intently as he began stroking himself. He put his other hand on the wall beside my head, bracing himself, and leaned in to kiss me. He then brushed his lips across my ear.

"Allie," he whispered. "You're unbelievable. I have never been as turned on as I am with you."

I brought the Waterpik closer, practically numbing myself with the intense spray. I felt him against my leg as he stroked faster, bringing himself to the edge.

"I want you to come on me," I said.

"Allie...."

"Matt...I'm going to come..."

Matt pulled away slightly to get a better view, watching as I opened myself even more, using an expert touch with the showerhead to bring myself to orgasm. He pulled back further and braced himself against the wall again as he came across my belly and my breasts. I handed him the showerhead and picked up the shower gel, lathering it up in my hands before washing myself and letting him rinse.

We dried each other off with the fluffiest towels we'd touched in five months. It was heavenly. We were giggling like teenagers as we made our way towards the kitchen, praying Trish had left some snacks in the fridge. Matt had his towel wrapped around his waist as he scoured around. I sat down at the kitchen table, content to let him forage while I went through the massive piles of mail. Who even sent mail anymore?

"Cheese sandwich?" Matt asked.

"Sounds great," I said, getting back to the mail.

Bills, fliers, subscription renewals, menus, a few New Year's cards, *a lot* of Christmas cards, and then one plain, white envelope with very familiar handwriting, simply addressed to me. I flipped it over to see the return address.

It was from Josh.

I quickly tucked the envelope into the middle of one of the piles as Matt came to the table with one plate bearing two sandwiches.

He smiled and kissed me as he sat down and handed me a sandwich.

"Happy?" he asked.

"Never been happier."

Other books by Sydney Campbell:

Allie Styles Romance Series:
Temptation (Book 1)
Deception (Book 2)
Reckonings (Book 3)
Beginnings (Book 4)

Courtyard Tales of Contemporary Romance
Reawakening
Redemption
Reckless